Praise for Raina James's
Three Wicked Wishes

"*Three Wicked Wishes* is a fun, erotic, romantic romp. Raina James has done a wonderful job of character development with Cassie and David—creating two characters that are lovable, fun, and flawed—very realistic and true to life."

~ *Fresh Fiction*

"I enjoyed the premise of this story very much, it's nice to come across something a little different in the erotic romance genre. [...] A good novel, nice characters, realistic but magical, enough between the sheets action to stoke the fire and a lovely ending."

~ *Long and Short Reviews*

Look for these titles by
Raina James

Now Available:

Love in a Bottle
Three Wicked Wishes

Three Wicked Wishes

Raina James

SAMHAIN
PUBLISHING

Samhain Publishing, Ltd.
11821 Mason Montgomery Road, 4B
Cincinnati, OH 45249
www.samhainpublishing.com

Three Wicked Wishes
Copyright © 2013 by Raina James
Print ISBN: 978-1-61921-420-0
Digital ISBN: 978-1-61921-255-8

Editing by Christa Desir
Cover by Kanaxa

First Samhain Publishing, Ltd. electronic publication: October 2012
First Samhain Publishing, Ltd. print publication: December 2013

Dedication

To Morgan Ashbury, Lara Santiago and Emma Wildes, and the totally stupendous writers' retreat on Kiawah Island, where they told me *Three Wicked Wishes* did sound like a fun story and, heck, yeah, I should write it. Ladies, here it is. Enjoy!

Chapter One

Cassandra trudged into the office, hair dripping, face red, stylish new black trench coat covered in a layer of orange cat hair.

Ensconced behind the semicircular desk at Reception, Michelle stared wide-eyed. "Cassie! What happened to you?"

She held up her hand, stop-sign fashion, and kept going. "Don't ask." The heavy black satchel started to slide off her shoulder. With an irritated jerk, she settled the wide strap back in place, trying not to wince as her stockinged feet squished wetly in her black leather wedge heels.

"Mr. Michalek said you're to join him in conference room B when you're settled."

Cassie stopped walking. Her shoulders slumped. *Shit.* The conference call with Baltimore. With everything else going on this morning, she'd forgotten all about it. She slid up the cuff of her trench coat and looked at the slim gold watch her parents had given her on her graduation from business college. Almost thirty-five minutes late, which meant the conference call started fifteen minutes ago.

"He didn't seem angry," Michelle said in an obvious effort to make her feel better. Cassie glanced over her shoulder to see the other woman on her feet, leaning forward over the high shelf of the reception desk. On Michelle, the cordless headset for the phones looked like a fashion accessory. Her milkmaid-pretty cheeks, auburn hair pulled into a sleek twist and wide, deep-blue eyes made Cassie even more aware of her own drowned-rat state. "Really," Michelle said. "When I told him you called to say you had car trouble, he said he'd see if Richardson's EA could take notes until you got in."

"Great," Cassie said, trying to mean it as she started to escape to her cubicle.

"Uh, Cassie? Maybe you should swing by the ladies' room on your way." Michelle gestured discreetly at her own eyes with the tips of her fingers.

Wonderful. Did she have raccoon eyes? "Thanks."

"Hey, what are friends for? Are we still on for lunch, or do you need to work through again?"

"Unless David needs me for something specific, we're definitely on. After the morning I've had, I'm in dire need of some of Petrelli's lemon mousse."

Michelle nodded sympathetically. "I hear you."

With a sad attempt at a cheerful wave, Cassie tightened her grip on the strap of her satchel and headed for the ladies' room. Her nylons clung damply to her legs and she tried to remember if she had a spare package in her desk. She kept her head down and tried to send out don't-talk-to-me vibes. She sensed heads turning and her coworkers' stares as she trudged through the maze of cubicles and past the breakroom.

Pushing through the door to the ladies' room, she almost collided with Amber Pilecky. The woman's eyes widened in surprise, then lit with barely contained laughter.

"Omigod, Cassie," her nemesis purred. "I almost didn't recognize you."

"Hello, Amber." Cassie tried to go around, but the other woman casually placed a hand on the wall, blocking her.

"But then I saw that distinctive wrinkle between your eyes and I knew it had to be you."

Cassie resisted—barely—the urge to glare. She couldn't help it. Amber always brought out the worst in her. "That's not a wrinkle; I'm just trying not to sneeze. Must be your perfume or something."

"I'm sure." Amber smirked. Her skillfully applied makeup and the thick waves of her shoulder-length, pale blonde hair made Cassie feel even more bedraggled than Michelle's prettiness had. It didn't help that Amber was her least favorite person in the universe. The dislike had been instant and mutual upon their meeting a few years before when Amber arrived at the company like one of the popular kids gracing the losers with her presence. Of course, Amber got along with the male employees a lot better than she did with the women.

"Doesn't Mr. Roland need you to make him coffee, answer the phone, or bend over to pick up a pencil?"

"Not at all. Rolly," Amber said, using the diminutive usually reserved for the chief executive's cronies, "prefers just a bottle of water when he's on a conference call. Say," she said, thoughtfully tapping one perfectly manicured nail on her bottom lip, "aren't you supposed to be in on that?"

Cursing under her breath, Cassie shoved past Roland's office bauble. As the bathroom door closed, she heard Amber's mocking laugh and gritted her teeth.

What she saw in the mirror made her want to groan. God, it was worse than she'd suspected. Her mascara was waterproof, so hadn't run. The good news ended there. Her eyeliner, once applied in an artfully thin stroke on her upper lid to emphasize her leaf-green eyes, had morphed into black blotches Alice Cooper would have envied. Rosy cheeks that made Michelle look like a sweet young thing gave Cassie's paler complexion an almost clownish appearance. Where it wasn't slicked to her head like ratty dreadlocks, her golden brown hair frizzed in a pouffy corona barely contained by the gold clip at the base of her neck.

Slinging her satchel onto the counter, Cassie took off the trench coat and tossed it over her bag. Water darkened the collar of her sage-green shirt. A number of splotch marks marred the fabric where water had soaked through her coat. Her nipples formed ice-cube-hard points visible even through the lace of her bra and the delicate cami she wore under the thin blouse. So much for dressing to play down her generous breasts.

She thought of the vengeance she'd like to wreak on the driver of the SUV that had roared through the puddle under the McCarthy Street overpass. Puddle didn't do it justice. It was typical of her luck to reach that section of road at the exact moment when the heavy downpour overwhelmed the storm sewers to form a minilake in the dip in the road. With water lapping midway up the hubcaps, it was enough to bog down her little Camry, a Prius and a boat of a Malibu. Hoping to assess just how bad the damage was, Cassie opened her car door in time to get a faceful of rooster tail as the SUV powered through like a kajillion-horsepower speedboat. The other stranded drivers were sympathetic but unhelpful as they waited for the tow trucks to arrive. She'd have to call the garage when she got a moment and find out how much it would cost to make her drowned little car roadworthy again. Hopefully, all it needed was drying out.

Sighing, she unbuttoned her blouse and slipped it off. A convulsive shudder racked her, then subsided into shivers. Gooseflesh pebbled her skin. The water dripping down her spine from her sopping-wet hair didn't help. Waving her hand under the motion-sensitive dryer to get it going, Cassie held her blouse under the blast of hot air. The warmth soon eased her shivers and she anticipated sliding the fabric back on. When it was mostly dry, she hung the blouse on a hook in one of the toilet stalls. She looked at her watch and grimaced. She'd lost another ten minutes.

Going back to the counter, she avoided her reflection and turned the faucet on as hot as she could stand it. Pumping a scanty froth of bubbles from the soap dispenser into her palm, she hurriedly scrubbed her face free of makeup. The best she could do with her hair was brush it out and plait it in a French braid, securing it with a hair elastic she kept in her bag for emergencies. Lastly, she put the blouse back on. It had lost its crispness, but at least she was warm enough she wouldn't be embarrassed by the nipple alert.

Cassie grabbed her satchel and coat and slammed out of the ladies' room, almost running to her cubicle. Dumping her things in her chair, she opened her desk drawer to take out a tiny recorder, notepad and a pen.

She straightened and paused. Someone had left a pretty little box on her desk.

Positioned in the center of her blotter, the shiny red box bound with a gold ribbon looked out of place amidst the orderly arrangement of files, computer monitor, multiline phone, manual Rolodex and other office paraphernalia. A touch of whimsy in a tableau of the everyday. Clutching her notepad to her chest, Cassie picked up the box. About the size of a coffee mug, it felt solid, but not too heavy. Turning it this way and that, she searched for a tag or label, but couldn't find one. What was it? Who had left it on her desk? It wasn't her birthday.

A burst of laughter from the direction of the breakroom startled her from her musings. Her eyes went to the clock on her monitor. Crap. No time to puzzle over it now. She put the box back on her blotter and hurried to conference room B. Without knocking, she eased open one of the oversized doors and slid into the room.

One of the managers stood at the head of the table, using an LED pointer to indicate something on a chart on the easel at his side. A slim wall-mounted monitor mirrored his move as it displayed the feed going out to the senior managers gathered in a similar conference room in Baltimore. The dozen or so executives around the table either watched the presentation or took notes.

Cassie's eyes met David's. Another shiver went through her, this one owing nothing to her chill. He had the whole Clark Kent, sexy-geek thing going on—black hair just long enough for a slight curl, intelligent blue eyes and sharp-planed features that were saved from austerity by the almost lush bow of his lips. It was easy to imagine bulging biceps and washboard abs under the well-tailored business suit. He even wore glasses, though the thin gold frames were nothing like the Man of Steel's horn rims. At the moment, his blue eyes seemed almost black behind the shining lenses, which reflected the glow of the wall-mounted monitor in the dim room. Cassie, certain the twitch of his lips indicated his amusement at her appearance, felt her cheeks flush. "Sorry I'm late," she mouthed.

David tipped his head and gave a tiny shrug she took to mean it was no big deal.

Seeing Shelby, Larry Richardson's executive assistant, seated in one of the chairs placed against the wall by the door, Cassie joined her. Sharing a smile of greeting, Cassie clicked on her recorder and flipped open her notebook.

Officially, Cassie worked for Stockton Enterprises. The company started out as a publishing house. Over four decades, it expanded to newspapers and magazines, eventually broadening its scope to include a number of small TV stations.

It even ventured into producing television documentaries, but that was still a miniscule part of the business.

Now, the company was looking to expand yet again.

The media business was a tough one. As anyone who knew anything about the business understood, diversification was key. No one specialized anymore. That way led to extinction. With the number of newspaper organizations failing in the United States, it was vital that Stockton Enterprises reinvent itself.

That was where David Michalek came in. David was a corporate consultant. His expertise lay in assessing a company's strengths and weaknesses; specifically, how to minimize the weaknesses and capitalize on the strengths to use them to their best advantage.

His job was to map out a plan for Stockton's future and make it a paying one. He was damn good at it too. Cassie felt privileged to have been tapped to serve as his aide-de-camp while he worked on Stockton's restructuring.

The plan had been for Cassie to fill in while David searched for a replacement for his executive assistant, who was on leave of absence to help her daughter with a new baby. Instead, after just a few days, he requested that Cassie be assigned to him for the duration. She was thrilled at the chance to work with David on implementing his ambitious plan, which included reorganization as well as the purchase of several other businesses as he took Stockton to the next level—online.

It was an incredible thing to be a part of. Finally, she felt like she was getting some use out of her dusty business degree. She'd learned a lot working with David.

Cassie checked her recorder to make sure it was on and tried to focus on what the presenter was saying so she could take notes. One of the things she liked best about David was his interest in her opinion. He really seemed to value her impressions.

Unwillingly, her eyes strayed to him. He sat back in his chair, hands folded in a relaxed manner on his stomach. Despite the casual posture, she had no doubt his attention was complete. His expression serious, he nodded in understanding as the man wrapped up his presentation. Clean-shaven cheeks emphasized the strong bone structure of his face.

The manager sat down at the table and the image on the screen changed to show the boardroom in Baltimore where eight men and women sat around a table. Cassie's pen scratched on her notepad as David spoke to the management team of the Baltimore multimedia firm Stockton had acquired under his direction, finishing with, "Okay, then. As soon as the new figures are ready, shoot them to Cassie."

The monitor clicked off and David stood. Cassie waited while he spoke with William Beasley, Stockton's vice-president of marketing, and Roland. At last, the men left, nodding hello to Cassie as they passed her at the door.

"David," she began. "I'm really sorry I was late."

He paused in stacking the few folders he'd brought into the meeting. "It's fine, Cassie. You know this stuff backwards and forwards anyway." He picked up the folders and walked to meet her. She fell in step as he led the way into the hall. "Michelle said you had car trouble?"

"Stalled out in the biggest puddle I've seen in my life. Anyway, I'll get started on the amendments to those spreadsheets. Is there anything else you want added to them?"

"Nothing we didn't discuss Friday."

They paused outside her cubicle. The sight of the mysterious red box made her frown.

David followed her gaze. "What's that?" he asked. "Is it your birthday?"

"No. I don't know what it is. It was on my desk when I got in."

"Maybe you have a secret admirer."

Something in David's voice drew her attention. His expression gave nothing away, yet she thought she saw a teasing glint in his eye.

"A secret admirer?" She forced a light laugh. "Wouldn't that be something?"

Cassie's computer bonged, signalling the arrival of an e-mail. In her most professional tone, she said, "That's probably the reports from Baltimore. I should print those up for you, then I need to work on the spreadsheets. And I also want to check with legal about those contracts you requested."

Tone wry, David said, "Well, don't let me keep you from your work. Just don't work too hard, all right?"

"Sure."

With a nod of farewell, he continued down the hall toward his office.

Cassie watched him go, her gaze lingering on the seat of his pants. Even through the fine fabric of his slacks, his butt cheeks looked round, firm and totally grabbable. She imagined how taut they'd feel under her fingers as she dug her nails in and held on. Shaking her head to dismiss the image and force her thoughts back on business, Cassie went into her cubicle.

Again, her eyes were drawn to the red box. Setting down her notepad and recorder, Cassie picked it up. Maybe it was meant for someone else and was put on her desk by mistake. With that thought in mind, Cassie went to the cubicle to the right of hers. There the occupant had made the space completely her own. Every inch of space not needed for work-related items was covered with photos of three children at various ages as well as a range of homemade crafts, from the ubiquitous macaroni art of kindergarten to sketches and doodles from more senior art classes.

A middle-aged woman sat at the desk, phone tucked between shoulder and chin as she typed on her keyboard. Long, professionally done acrylic nails painted rose pink made a *click-click* sound on the keys. Spying Cassie, the woman smiled and held up a finger to signal she'd be just a moment.

"Thanks, Lou. Got it. I'll make sure the updated information gets put in the system." She laughed at something the caller said. "Watch it, or I'll sic my husband on you." Still laughing, she dropped the handset back in the cradle. Turning to Cassie, she said, "He's been a total dog since his wife left him."

"You're telling me. Do you know how many times I've had to pretend I was going to the ladies' room because I saw he was in the breakroom and didn't want to get trapped in there with him? The puppy-dog eyes are killing me. Well, the puppy-dog eyes and the leer. Do you think they cancel each other out?"

Linda gave an exaggerated shudder. "Thank God he's seen my husband. Mike would break him in two if he stepped out of line with me. It's you single girls who should watch out for him."

"Your Mike's a sweetie. You've got a keeper there."

"Lucky me." Though she rolled her eyes, it was clear Linda was serious in the sentiment. "We really should report Lou to HR, you know."

"He's just so darn pathetic about it all. I haven't got the heart."

"Yeah, I guess. So what brings you to my little corner of the empire?"

Cassie held up the box. "I found this on my desk, but there's no tag on it or card. Since it's not my birthday or anything, I thought maybe someone put it on my desk by mistake."

"Well, it's not my birthday either, but I'd be happy to take it off your hands."

Feeling strangely possessive, Cassie clutched the box. "That's okay. Thought I'd ask, just to be sure. Did you see anyone go into my cubicle to drop it off?"

"Sorry, hon. I've been on and off the phone since I got in. I wouldn't have noticed Brad Pitt if he dropped it off."

Cassie grinned. "I know the feeling. Today was going to be a killer as it was, and now I'm really behind the eight ball."

Linda quirked a brow. "Oh? What's up?"

Cassie heard the distant *bong* of her computer as another e-mail arrived. "Geez. I swear, e-mail's worse than a ringing phone. I've really got a lot of catching up to do, Linda. I'll have to fill you in later."

"Sure thing."

Cassie hurried back into her cubicle. She itched to open the box, but even as she had the thought, another *bong* sounded. Biting her lip, she looked from the box to the flashing message window on her monitor. Then she thought of everything she had to get done today. If she fell behind, it would snowball on her for the rest of the week. Before she could decide against doing the right thing, she stuffed the ribbon-wrapped box into her satchel, hoping that out of sight would be out of mind.

She'd just have to open it later when she had a few minutes to spare. She thought of David's words. Secret admirer, indeed. With her luck, it was Freaky Harold from the mailroom. Or Leering Lou.

Cassie put the bag on the floor beside her desk and resolutely turned to her computer.

Chapter Two

It was almost nine by the time Cassie fumbled the key into the lock and let herself into her building's entryway. A crystal chandelier mounted on the vaulted ceiling high above lit the space. The wood-slab floor gleamed with the glow of a recent polish. A row of antique-style, metal mailboxes, also showing the signs of the landlady's diligent care, hung from the wall on the right. Automatically, Cassie flipped open the lid of her mailbox and scooped out the usual assortment of bills and flyers. Without even looking at them, she let the lid fall shut, stuffed the handful in the side pocket of her satchel and headed for the stairs.

Before her foot touched the first tread, a low growl stopped her. She peered down the short hall. There was one apartment on the main level, and that belonged to her elderly landlady, Dorothea Baintree. Hercules, Mrs. Baintree's psychotic marmalade tom, crouched on the welcome mat in front of the cat door cut into the rich wood panel of the apartment's door. Tail swishing, he watched Cassie with one slitted gold eye. He'd lost the other in a fight with some other cat. Or maybe in a deal with Satan. Cassie wouldn't put anything past the fickle creature. She glared back. It was because of Hercules that her new black coat sported a layer of orange hair.

While leaving for work, she'd noticed him huddled miserably under a shrub in the front yard, cold rain plastering his fur to his large, muscled body. The gemlike eye, as soulful as a cartoon kitten's, drew her reluctantly to his aid. He had a talent for that—appearing innocent and cutely appealing, then without warning transforming into a demon spawn frothing at the mouth, missing only the horns and forked tail. She never learned. This morning, she took time she didn't have to coax him from under the shrub and get him into the house. Then, as she'd half-known he would, when she got the front door open he turned into a biting, hissing, scratching ball of motion, digging his claws into her chest as he used it for a springboard to launch himself down the hallway. With a final disgruntled hiss, he'd disappeared through the cat door to be coddled and cooed over by Mrs. Baintree, whom Cassie had always found to be a fine, discerning woman, save for her choice in pets.

Cassie stuck her tongue out at Hercules and started up the stairs.

Her apartment was one of six in the massive, converted Victorian-style house. Mrs. Baintree's rooms were on the first floor; the second held three smallish apartments; and Cassie lived in one of the two apartments in what used to be the attic. Normally she didn't mind the climb up to the third level. The rich gloss of the dark wood paneling on the walls in the stairwell, the mingled scent of polish and old wood, the faint creak of the treads as she moved up them, the fading sound of the traffic on the street outside—like a half-remembered dream, it all somehow managed to convey a sense of another time and place far removed from her everyday, unexciting life. Now, it just felt like a long haul after an even longer day.

With a weary sigh, Cassie gripped the round newel post at the top of the stairs to haul herself up the last two steps—only to crash into a lean male chest.

Cassie's foot missed the step, her hand slipped off the post and she felt herself teeter. Before she could let out more than a squawk of fear, strong hands caught her elbows, steadied her, and pulled her the rest of the way up. She found herself nose-to-chest with an expensively cut suit coat, silk tie and crisp white shirt.

She looked up to see a chisel-faced blond stranger staring back at her with an expression of mingled apology and relief.

"Oh my God, Cassie! Are you all right?"

Feeling dazed after the adrenaline surge of the near miss, Cassie looked at the woman peering at her from around the *GQ* cover model.

"Cassie?"

Realizing her mouth hung open like a landed fish, Cassie snapped it shut. "What?" The word came out on a breath of air. She cleared her throat and tried again. "Oh. Fine. Yeah, I'm fine, Sarah. How are you?"

She briefly closed her eyes at the inanity. She felt the blood rush to her cheeks, which had likely been paper white from shock. It didn't ease her embarrassment when Sarah giggled, the sound as sweet as bells chiming. Cassie liked her across-the-hall neighbor, she really did, but sometimes the gorgeous redhead was just too perfect to bear.

Geez, the couple looked like they'd walked off the set of *Beautiful People*. Was that even a show? Didn't matter—if there was such a thing, this pair would have starring roles in it. A slinky blue dress showed off Sarah's body to perfection, the silky fabric clinging to the dips and curves, except where it plunged between her breasts, exposing the sensuous slopes. Sarah had the confidence to pull off the little-bit-of-nothing dress like *she* accented *it*, not the other way around.

The blond guy in the suit was admittedly droolworthy. Wowzers. David Michalek was the man of Cassie's dreams, but she wasn't dead. Scratch that. This guy looked like he had enough going on in all departments to raise the happy hormones of the dead with a crook of one lean, strong finger.

Speaking of which... Cassie looked down at the hands that still gripped her elbows. He seemed to realize it at the same moment, because with a murmured, "Sorry," he dropped her and wrapped an arm possessively around Sarah's slim waist.

Sarah smiled at him like he was a puppy who'd come when called, then turned the smile on Cassie. "I forgot. You haven't met Kyle yet, have you? We were just going out for a late supper."

No, Cassie hadn't met Kyle yet. And really, would it matter? Sarah was very particular about the men she dated, but also very firm about not tying herself down to any one man. Who knew if Kyle would be around long enough to get to know?

Cassie pretended not to notice as Kyle discreetly plucked an orange cat hair off his well-tailored sleeve and flicked it away.

Of course, Sarah *would* have a hot date on a Monday night. She could have a hot date every night of the week if she wanted, and often did. Cassie envied her friend her options. "Sounds like fun," she said.

Sarah, brow knit in a beautiful, concerned frown, touched Cassie's arm. "Are you sure you're all right?"

"Of course! You go ahead to dinner. I'm perfectly okay, now that my heart rate can't give a gerbil a run for its money."

"Would you like to join us? We're going to try out that new sushi place everyone's talking about. You should come. You don't mind, do you, Kyle?" She looked up at the blond god and curved her lips in a promise of good things to come if he went along with her.

Cassie gave him points for squelching most of the dismay in his voice when he said, "No, not at all. We'd be happy to have you join us."

Cassie swallowed a snort. "You're sweet to ask, Sarah, but all I want right now is to put my feet up and relax."

"Well," Sarah said slowly. "If you're sure—"

"I'm sure. You go. Have fun."

Kyle didn't wait for Cassie to change her mind. He hustled Sarah down the stairs with a hurried, "Good night." The *click-click* of Sarah's stilettos on the wooden treads faded.

Cassie shook her head. She had to laugh at herself. Sarah was off to be wined and dined by one truly fine piece of man, while the best Cassie could anticipate was a night in front of the TV before crawling into bed alone. Typical.

Cassie fit her key into the lock and let herself into her apartment. She closed the door behind her and kicked off her shoes. The cute leather wedges definitely looked the worse for wear after their soaking this morning. Switching the strap of her bag from one hand to the other, she worked her cat-hair-dusted coat off. Maybe a tumble in the dryer would get rid of the worst of the hair. She sighed, giving it up for the moment. She didn't have the energy to trek down to the laundry room. About to dump the coat on top of the shoes, she stopped and conscientiously hung it in the closet so it wouldn't clutter up her small apartment.

What she called cozy, her mother termed a shoebox. Cassie loved it. The galley kitchen suited her just fine. It wasn't like she was a master chef. And sure, the living room looked crowded with the cute little two-seater table she ate at, her single love seat, comfy chair and footstool. So her bedroom was a bit cramped with her high-mattress double bed and the matching dresser. The bathroom, however, was to die for. The old-fashioned claw-foot tub had sold her on the apartment. Cassie thought longingly of the tub and considered running herself a decadent bubble bath. Whiling away a few hours with a bottle of wine and a steamy novel was a tempting lure. It was

25

after nine and she really was beat. She'd be better off catching a bite to eat, watching a bit of tube and heading to bed like a good little girl.

Hah. Good little girl. Like she had a choice. But being bad like Sarah was far more enticing at the moment.

Maybe if she had a warm body to come home to, it would be more appealing. Like a cat, a sweet-tempered one nothing like Hercules. She grimaced. God, a single woman getting a cat to keep her company. Could she be any more of a cliché? Scratch the cat idea.

"Suck it up, buttercup," she murmured. Pausing to drop her bag on the oversized footstool that doubled as her coffee table, Cassie went into her bedroom to yank off her work clothes. Her nylons, the toes and heels stained black with shoe dye, went right in the garbage can. Tossing the rest of her clothes in the hamper, Cassie pulled on soft flannel sleeping pants and a roomy, well-washed sweatshirt with the faded ghost of her alma mater's mascot on the front. A thick pair of cotton socks and her favorite fuzzy slippers completed her attire.

In the kitchen area, the first thing she did was pour a big glass of red wine from the pricey bottle in the fridge. Wine was something she didn't economize on, though she was heathen enough to like her red chilled. She took a big sip and immediately felt a little better about her day. It was almost over. In short order, she prepared herself a plate of cheese cubes, grapes, a sliced apple and a couple of pieces of French bread spread with soft herb cheese.

Cassie carried her plate and glass to her comfy chair and settled in with the TV remote. The screen filled with a colorful cartoon intro accompanied by a bouncy, pseudo-Arabian theme with a sixties beat. "*I Dream of Jeannie*! I haven't seen this in forever."

Note to self: Stop talking to self.

The silly vintage comedy was irresistible. Cassie sipped her wine and chuckled along with the canned laugh track. Barbara Eden as the sexy-sweet genie, Jeannie, quickly embroiled the perennially high-strung Tony in yet another scrape. As she watched, the beleaguered astronaut and his buddy, Roger, dove into a garbage chute at NASA. She narrowed her eyes. Larry Hagman really was pretty handsome way back when.

Admittedly, clean-cut, all-American guys usually did it for her. Guys like David, who would probably laugh his ass off if he found out how she felt about him. Not that she'd ever act on it. Getting involved with someone you worked with was just plain dumb. The heartache when the relationship ended, as she knew from a past experience, was a bitch when you still had to see the guy at work, day in and day out. Besides, David Michalek was just so together, while she was a bit of a ditz. Talk about an odd couple.

Time to think about something else.

She stifled a yawn. The wine and food were making her a bit sleepy. Too, it had been a long, exhausting day. David had looked especially yummy today. The silvery-blue tie he'd paired with a pale blue shirt brought out silver sparks in his solemn blue eyes. Hey, she could decide he was off-limits as far as a relationship, but she wasn't blind. A little fantasizing never hurt anyone.

Cassie smiled dreamily, unfolded her legs and stretched them out on the ottoman. Her slippered foot kicked her bag, pushing it out of the way to make room. As she watched through half-closed eyes, the bag reached the tipping point. Before it slid to the floor, a familiar red box with a fancy gold ribbon spurted out of the bag's gaping mouth. It wobbled a bit beside her feet as the bag hit the floor with a solid *thump*.

Cassie sat up, the quick movement sloshing wine over her hand. "Hey! I forgot all about that." Now that she thought about it, it was kind of strange that the box hadn't crossed her mind since she'd stuffed it in her bag this morning. It wasn't every day she got an anonymous gift of any kind, let alone a classy one that looked like it came from an expensive chocolatier or jeweler.

She put the wineglass down on the petite end table between the chair and love seat and licked the pleasantly tart liquid off her fingers. She picked up the box and turned it in her hands. She inspected the underside for a logo or writing to give her some clue about where it came from. Nothing. She held it to one ear and gave it a little shake. Again, nothing. It felt solid, but not really heavy.

"Only one way to find out." Cassie tugged on one end of the ribbon. The bow unraveled with the glide of heavy satin and fell to her lap. She eased the lid up with her thumbs. There, nestled in a bed of gold tissue paper, was a cut-crystal bottle half-filled with a pearly liquid.

Cassie gasped. It was beautiful. Carefully, she lifted the bottle out of the box. In the blue glow cast by the TV, the liquid sparkled with tiny flecks of gold, silver and the fiery sparks of opal. She wondered what it was. It didn't look like any perfume she'd ever seen, though the style of bottle seemed to indicate that's what it was. She touched the bulb of crystal at the top of the bottle. It moved loosely under her fingertip. But that couldn't be. If it weren't secure, the liquid in the bottle would have leaked out all over the tissue paper, especially considering the way she'd shaken the box and the less-than-careful journey home in her satchel.

Carefully, she plucked at the crystal bulb. It slid easily from the top of the bottle, bringing with it a slender stem, glossy with liquid. She sniffed it, expecting to detect an earthy musk or the scent of exotic flowers. Instead, it seemed to be odorless.

As Cassie watched, a thick drop of liquid formed on the tip of the glass stem. It swelled larger as more liquid trickled down the stem and joined the drop. The surface of the tiny ball of liquid quivered in eerie tandem with the beat of her heart. Gravity took over. The drop fell away from the stem. It landed with a small plop on the thin skin of her inner wrist.

Suddenly, the air filled with everything she'd expected to detect when she first opened the bottle: the earthy musk of midnight kisses; the brush of petals over skin sensitized by just the right amount of loving; the sweet, succulent sugar of mangoes and peaches and fruits she couldn't name.

Cassie sucked in an involuntary breath of wonder and delight—and promptly lost it in a *whoosh* of shock when a stranger's voice said, "Packs a punch, doesn't it?"

Chapter Three

Cassie almost dropped the bottle.

She juggled it in her hand a moment before managing to get the crystal stopper back in place. It was hard to concentrate on her coordination when a strange woman appeared to be making herself at home on Cassie's love seat.

The stranger wore black leather pants, spiky black heels and a soft purple sweater that emphasized the golden tint of her skin and thick-lashed, tip-tilted brown eyes. Blue-black hair tumbled in sleep-tousled curls around an exotically gorgeous face and spilled down the woman's shoulders to her elbows.

She rested her arms along the top of the love seat and crossed one knee over the other. Her heel-shod foot bounced to some unheard beat.

"One of the top male fantasies going. Well, that and Princess Leia-Slave Girl. Or Jeannie *and* Princess Leia-Slave Girl."

"Wha—?"

The woman nodded at the TV where Major Tony stomped around on the white-sand beach of an apparently deserted island, screaming at Jeannie to get him out of there. The screen cut to the bouncy blonde in a red-and-pink harem outfit, sprawled in the cushioned elegance of her magic bottle. Her pose bore an eerie resemblance to that of the woman currently sprawled in Cassie's living room.

"A Jeannie harem fantasy, minus the cute blouse under the jacket and with a few strategic body piercings. One of my top sellers. Go figure. I'd take Princess Leia-Slave Girl, myself."

Cassie gaped at the woman. "Who *are* you? And what are you doing in my apartment?" Her head swiveled from the stranger to the front door and back. "*How* did you get in my apartment?"

"I'm the genie of the bottle, sweetie."

"Uh-huh. I think you need to leave. I'd really hate to have to call the police." To herself, she mumbled, "Must have drifted off, or something."

"Nope, sorry," the woman said. "You're wide awake, sweetie, and I didn't wander through your door while you were in La-La Land. I suppose you could call the police, but it would be so embarrassing—for you—when they showed up and there was no one here but you and the dust bunnies."

"Dust bunnies! Look, I keep a clean house." Honesty forced her to add, "Mostly."

The woman looked pointedly at the teetering stack of romance novels perched on the shelf, but limited her response to, "You can call me Jane."

"Jane. Right." Cassie closed her eyes. She put the perfume bottle back in the box on her lap, then held the bridge of her nose between thumb and forefinger. The intriguing scent of the droplet on her wrist tickled her nostrils. "I'm dreaming. I was watching *I Dream of Jeannie* and fell asleep. Maybe the wine went bad in the fridge, or the cheese—I *knew* I shouldn't have splurged on that nonpasteurized stuff—and that's why I'm having a really weird, bizarre, freako dream."

The woman laughed, pure sex in the throaty sound. "Keep thinking that, doll."

Cassie took a few fortifying breaths. Then a few more. She listened, hard. All she could hear was the patter of the sitcom on the TV and the distant, very distant, sound of a car driving by on the street three stories below. She pinched the skin on the back of one hand and bit back a cheeping sound at the sharp pain. Yup. She was awake. Cautiously, she opened her eyes.

The woman on the love seat waggled her fingers at Cassie in a cutesy wave. "Still here," she said. "And, no, you're not dreaming."

She spoke with the nonregional accent perfected by TV newscasters across North America, but there was something undeniably different about Jane's voice. Cassie couldn't pin it down. Not that it mattered, since she'd lost her mind and all.

"Okay." Cassie picked up her glass and bolted down the last of her wine like a hardened drunk slugging back a shot of whiskey. "It's finally happened. I've gone crazy. Nuts. Certifiable." Staring wistfully at the dregs of wine in the glass, she moaned. "I bet that witch Amber is going to laugh her skinny ass off when she finds out." *And then she'll seduce David, just like she's always wanted.* That thought made Cassie tip the glass to her mouth, trying to catch the last of the wine with her tongue.

"Back up the crazy train, Cassandra," Jane said. "You're not dreaming, you're not nuts, and this is really happening. Believe it."

"Well, excuse me if you don't look like any genie I've ever seen."

"Oh, you mean like this?" Jane snapped her fingers. From one blink to the next, she went from lounging on the love seat in leather and angora to hovering over a brass, Aladdin-style lamp, wearing nothing more than strings of jewels and transparent purple veils. Not one part of her body touched the floor. Cassie's jaw dropped. With a jangle of gold bracelets, Jane snapped her fingers again. Away went the veils and lamp. The supple leather pants barely made a sound as Jane settled back on the love seat, propped her heels on the ottoman and crossed her long legs at the ankles.

"What is it with people? Always with the theatrics," she said. "Sorry to disappoint you, Princess Jasmine, but I don't do a song-and-dance routine with an elephant and a flying carpet with language issues." Jane muttered something that sounded like, "Damn that Disney guy, anyway."

"All right, Jane. Let's say I believe you. You're a genie." Cassie was proud of herself for not stumbling over the word. "The genie of the bottle." Swallowing the half-nervous, half-hysterical titter was harder. "Why are you here?"

"To make all your dreams come true," Jane said in a low, melodramatic voice with an obviously exaggerated accent that sounded like a B-movie Dracula.

"I *knew* it was a dream!"

Jane sighed. "Try to have a little fun... No, Cassandra, you are not dreaming. I'm here, you're here. Get the picture?"

"Then let me repeat: Why are you here?"

Jane twirled a lock of midnight-black hair around one finger, the nail of which had been shaped into a perfect oval painted a pretty shell pink. "Your three wishes, of course."

Cassie didn't know what to say. *Wishes?* Jane continued in a businesslike tone, "Let's talk ground rules."

"Sure. Let's."

"First, you've gotta understand I'm not your usual sort of genie."

"Oh, I can believe that."

Jane's brow quirked, as if she detected Cassie's thinly shaded sarcasm, but chose to ignore it. "I cater to a special kind of...we'll call them 'clients'."

Cassie nodded.

"Forget about fame, fortune, world peace—my wishes are much more personal in nature. Intimate. Your deepest, darkest desires."

Again, Cassie nodded. When Jane didn't elaborate, she prompted, "So that means...?"

"Silly woman! I will make your fantasies a reality." Jane folded her arms across her impressive chest with a self-satisfied nod, as if that explained everything.

"Fantasies. But I don't have any fantasies."

Jane snorted. "Sweetie, I *know* what you were thinking about your neighbor's hunk of the week. Kyle, wasn't it?"

Cassie felt the blood rush to her face in a mortified blush. "So? He was attractive. I can admit it. So what? Besides, I barely even thought..."

Jane offered a sly, knowing smile. "Gotta hand it to you, Cass, you sure can pack a lot of action into a few seconds of prurient thoughts."

"Oh, for the love of—"

"Not that I'm complaining. Professionally speaking, I like creative thinkers. It makes things so much more interesting." Before Cassie could stutter another protest, Jane waved her hand in a dismissive gesture. "Anyway, back to business. Your wishes."

"Wishes. Right. By all means, let's get to the wishes."

Everything went dim. Cassie's stomach lurched as though she'd just started the downward plunge of a skyscraper-tall roller coaster. Her eardrums vibrated unpleasantly and pressure seemed to press in on her. She could clearly see the glow of the television and the shine of light from the kitchen, but it was as if everything were far away, seen through a rain-fogged window.

Only one thing in the room was crystal clear: Jane. She seemed to glow with an inner light. In a matter of breaths, everything in the room took on a purple tint. Dark chocolate eyes flared to blazing amber, holding Cassie enthralled.

When Jane spoke, magic and mystery flowed through her words.

"Cassandra Eloise Parker." The name sounded strange and wonderful as Jane intoned it. "You are the holder of the sacred flask.

"Cassandra Eloise Parker." Cassie quivered at the repetition of her name. Her blood raced with an unfamiliar excitement and the pressure on her eardrums built. "You have been anointed with the oil of dreams, that which is reserved for a chosen few.

"Cassandra Eloise Parker." The syllables swirled in Cassie's mind as Jane demanded in a smoky voice that touched something deep inside her: "What is your deepest, most secret, most treasured desire?"

Cassie gasped. Convulsively, her fingers sank into the arms of the chair as a searing wave of desire swamped her senses. Her belly clenched, her thighs tightened and moisture drenched her cleft as her clit vibrated with sensation. A ragged cry tore from her throat.

Speechless, disoriented and weak as a kitten from the force of the unexpected orgasm, Cassie dropped her chin and tried to catch her breath. Her heart raced in her chest as if she'd spent hours in bed, with the world's most skilled lover steadily driving her toward the most earth-shattering orgasm she'd had in her life—or so she imagined. Shakily, she lifted a hand and pushed brunette curls away from her face. Too shattered to muster up more than a shred of embarrassment, Cassie lifted her eyes and met Jane's satisfied gaze.

"Got it," the genie said. "Three wishes, coming up."

And with a bawdy wink, she was gone.

Chapter Four

The sound of rain slapping against the windowpane woke her. Cassie groaned, vaguely surprised to find herself sprawled facedown on her bed wearing nothing more than a skimpy pair of cotton panties. At some point in the night she must have kicked off her sheet and blankets. Chill bumps raced over her bare flesh and she shivered. Her tongue felt like a lumpy wire scrub pad and her mouth tasted like sour, vinegary grapes, clueing her in that she hadn't brushed her teeth before going to bed. Slowly, she lifted her head, anticipating the pain of a hangover headache. Nothing. Her surprise turned to wonder. She'd swilled more than half a bottle of wine by herself last night. Not that it happened often, but when it did the morning after was almost always less than pleasant.

Last night.

In the morning light coming through the narrow dormer window, Cassie found it hard to believe what had happened. If it had even happened.

She thought again of all the wine she'd tipped back. Maybe, just possibly, she drank the wine before the genie "appeared". Far more likely that her wine-hazed mind, influenced by an *I Dream of Jeannie* marathon, had come up with some cracked genie fantasy than that a strange woman promising to fulfill Cassie's darkest sexual desires had appeared in her living room. In fact, the more Cassie considered it, the more plausible the first scenario seemed. Maybe she needed to lay off the Chilean stuff for a while. It was good, but if the wine brought on dreams like that, it wasn't worth it.

Already she felt some of the details of the wine-soaked dream—which had, just a few moments earlier, seemed so vivid—slipping away. All she could really remember about the strange woman was the most amazing pair of purple eyes. Or were they brown?

Cassie pushed herself to a half-sitting position and groggily tugged at the blankets mounded at the foot of her bed. Her eyes tracked to the ormolu clock on her dresser.

"Shit!"

Cassie launched herself off the bed and grabbed the clock, just to be sure her eyes weren't lying to her. Eight fifteen. She had forty-five minutes to get to work. And no car, she realized. Even if it was ready at the garage, there was no way she had time to swing by and pick it up. She couldn't be late for work two days in a row.

She thought of calling in sick. It wasn't like she did it very often, even when she *was* sick. But if she didn't go in to work, she wouldn't get to see David, talk to him, spend time with him.

Sad how her life had come down to aching for whatever scraps of attention she could get from the man who was her boss, even if just a temporary one. Semantics aside, he was off-limits, romantically speaking. Office romances were bad news, especially when there was a significant disparity between the positions of the people involved. Period. End of story. Cassie's thinking brain knew that, even if her brainless hormones didn't.

So she had to content herself with a satisfying work relationship. For that to happen, she had to actually make it in to work.

Resigned to the expense, she picked up the phone to call a cab. Forget breakfast, makeup and blow-drying her hair. She'd just have time to take a quick shower, throw on some clothes and get downstairs.

So far, Tuesday didn't appear to be starting out any better than Monday.

"Cassie, do you have plans for lunch today?"

She startled, then turned away from her computer screen to face the bearer of the too-sexy voice. David smiled. "Sorry, didn't mean to scare you."

Cassie's lips curved automatically in return, her heart racing from more than surprise. Just the sound of his deep, slightly rough voice made shivers run up her spine. Her nipples straightened like little soldiers under her blouse, making her glad of the wide decorative scarf draped around her shoulders and across her chest. She'd started adding scarves and sweaters to most of her office ensembles as soon as she realized the effect he had on her. In case she forgot, she kept an extra, neutral-toned scarf in her desk drawer. It was either that or buy granny lingerie guaranteed to be thick enough to flatten her eager nipples.

"So, lunch?"

She flushed. It was a wonder David didn't think she was scatterbrained, considering the number of times her mind wandered into inappropriate areas when he was around. "Lunch?" she parroted.

"Yes. Do you have plans?"

"No." Cassie fumbled on her desk to grab a notepad and pen. "I don't have any plans. What can I do for you?"

"Go to lunch with me."

Cassie, half out of her chair, stumbled. "Careful," he murmured, catching her forearm before she lost her balance entirely. His touch sent heat racing through her body and all her attention focused on his fingers cupping her arm. Cassie abruptly realized how close he stood. If she tipped her head up, her lips would graze his chin. His scent, a hint of rich cologne or soap over his own unique spice, teased her nostrils. When he stepped back to give her room to move, she sighed at the loss.

"Go to lunch? As in out somewhere?"

"Just around the corner," he said. "There's something I want to run by you."

"Okay. Sure thing. Just let me get my coat."

As casually as she could, Cassie put away her notebook and pen and got her purse out of her bottom drawer. She used her satchel to carry everything from granola bars and a compact umbrella, to a thick appointment book and a minipharmacy, and she hung her coat on a sturdy hook on the wall of her cubicle, but she always took her purse out of the bag and left it in the drawer. When she reached for her coat, David took it and helped her into it. Cassie hoped he didn't notice her awkwardness. The gentlemanly gesture was the sort of thing David Michalek did as a matter of course. There was nothing special about it.

David paused at the reception desk to tell Michelle they'd be back in an hour or so. He held the door for Cassie, but stopped her when she would have turned left toward the deli on the next corner.

"I made reservations at the Black Swan," he said.

"Oh. How nice." Cassie tried to sound blasé. The Swan was where the company's executives wined and dined their more important business associates. Cassie had eaten there as a treat when her parents or her sisters and their husbands came to visit. That David had made reservations for the two of them meant nothing; he probably just really enjoyed the food.

Fortunately, the rain had ended sometime after Cassie's mad dash into the building from her taxi. The sidewalk shone wetly, the pavement and interlocking stone as clean as if someone had taken a scrub brush and broom to it. The air smelled fresh. Pedestrians, many with either unbuttoned coats or no coats at all, thronged the sidewalk, taking advantage of the mild weather and warm sun.

"I'm glad the weather is sticking," David commented. He navigated the crush of people easily, using his deceptively solid bulk to keep the other pedestrians from crowding them. "Winter seemed to be hanging on forever."

"I thought you liked to ski." Cassie distinctly remembered David's trip just after Christmas. Jealousy had eaten at her as she'd imagined him on an intimate getaway with some woman. Later, she'd felt like a fool when he invited her to see some pictures he'd snapped. He made her giggle over some story about a drunken buddy, a slippery dash to the hot tub and a predawn visit to the emergency room with some hard-to-explain injuries. It turned out the trip was an annual one he took with his former college roommate and a few other guys.

"Might as well do something fun when the snow's on the ground," David said with a shrug. "I'm just as happy to water-ski instead."

"Oh, me too."

"You water-ski?"

Cassie blushed. High school had been over for a decade, yet here she was, agreeing with whatever some hunky guy said just to make him like her. She tried to recover. "Well, no. I wouldn't mind learning though. It looks like fun. And I like trying new things."

His lips spread in a slow smile as he looked down at her. "Me too."

Thankfully, they reached the restaurant and she didn't have time to get too flustered by what could not have possibly been a sexual innuendo.

David took her elbow and guided her up the short walkway to the entrance. The exterior of the Black Swan looked as classy as its namesake. Small frosted panes of glass broke the surface of the glossy ebony door. On either side, wide windows with gauzy curtains reflected the sunlight, making it difficult to see more than a glimpse of the tables and diners.

As soon as they stepped inside, an elegant ambiance of low-voiced conversation, discreet classical music and the clink of expensive flatware on china enveloped them. A coolly attractive woman greeted them cordially. As she walked away with Cassie and David's coats, a nattily dressed man behind what looked like an antique lectern gave them a smooth smile.

"Mr. Michalek," he said. "How nice to see you."

"Thank you, Paul."

"Your table is ready, sir. This way, please."

Cassie noted the glances thrown their way as they trailed after the maître d'. She didn't recognize anyone, but David greeted a few people by name. She focused on seating herself without dragging the tablecloth askew, distractedly requested an ice water when asked and pretended to peruse the menu. Still flustered, she settled on a salad. Cassie couldn't help thinking about why David had asked her to lunch. While they'd shared meals back at the office, this was the first time they'd actually gone out.

Fortunately, David kept the conversational ball rolling almost on his own. She commented in the appropriate places as he spoke briefly about work before asking about her car, how she enjoyed living in the city compared to growing up in a small town, whether she got to see her family often. Before she realized it, he'd drawn from her the admission that her car would be ready by the end of the day, she loved living in the city, even though she missed her friends and the slower pace of her hometown, and while she didn't get to see her family all that often, it was frequent enough to satisfy her just fine, thank you.

David laughed. "I think I sense some serious overtones in that."

"Don't get me wrong," Cassie said, setting her fork down beside her empty plate. "I love my family dearly. The problem is, there are certain expectations I'm not quite ready to meet."

"Expectations?"

As one server efficiently whisked away the plates from their meal, David declined dessert, but accepted coffee. Cassie thought wistfully of the white-chocolate, raspberry trifle she'd seen delivered to a nearby table. She settled for coffee.

"You said something about expectations?" David prompted.

Cassie stirred a portion of cream into the fragrant cup of coffee. "Definitely. Do you know how hard it is to be the eldest of three girls, but be the only one who's still unmarried and childless?"

"No. I can honestly say I don't know how hard that is."

She pointed her spoon at him. "Don't laugh. Talk about pressure, when every guy you share a cup of coffee with gets the inquisition as a prospective husband."

"Something I can look forward to?"

"What?" When he toasted her with his coffee cup, she flushed. "Slip of the tongue. I think you're safe, boss." She tacked the last word on deliberately, as a reminder to herself. "I just find it old-fashioned that my parents are so worried about my relationship status, or lack thereof."

"Nothing wrong with old-fashioned."

"Sure. Says the guy who isn't being trotted out in front of the neighbors like a good breeder during every visit home."

"Cassie, I think it's fairly safe to say that when a person, man or woman, reaches a certain age, their family starts to feel like it is their duty to play matchmaker."

"Oh, really? This sounds good. What matches has your family made for you?"

"How about going home for Thanksgiving, expecting to sit around the TV watching the game with your father, uncles and brothers, only to find out everyone's getting together at someone else's house? Add to that the fact no one told you, you wake up in an empty house, and along comes your sister-in-law's cousin's coworker, who loves football and cooking and is thrilled to watch the game with you? Now who's laughing?"

Cassie snorted through the hands she'd clapped over her mouth. "Sorry. All right, you win. My family hasn't gone quite that far yet."

"Oh, they will. Just give it time," he pronounced ominously, which set her to laughing again.

"It's not like we're old or anything," she said when she had control of herself. "I'm not even thirty."

"And I'm only thirty-three," he said. "But they do it because they care."

"Yeah, you're right." Cassie took a small sip from her cup, trying to make her coffee last a little longer. They'd been gone for more than an hour and really should be getting back. It was just nice to have David to herself for a change.

"Cassie, what are your plans for the future?"

"Plans?"

He chuckled. "Yes. The dreaded what-are-you-going-to-do-with-your-life question. Do you like your job? I know you have a business degree, but you haven't really pursued a career that would make full use of it. Why? You're quick, smart, a real intuitive thinker when it comes to planning. You could achieve a lot more than you are at Stockton."

Flattered by his assessment, but anxious that he somehow found her lack of ambition a disappointment, Cassie nibbled on her lip. "I think what it comes down to is I don't have the go-for-the-throat instinct that all great business people seem to have."

David grinned. "Oh? And I do?"

"You know you do."

"Okay, I can see your point."

The efficient server arrived to warm up their cups of coffee. As soon as he was gone, David looked at Cassie expectantly. "So you aren't quite into the messier aspects of business. That still leaves a lot of room for a woman with intelligence and goals."

Cassie fiddled with the linen napkin on her lap while he waited for her to answer. When she did, it was in a rush, putting into words what she never had before.

"The thing is, I really love what I do—now. I like figuring things out, coming up with solutions to make things better or streamlining a process to smooth out the bumps. I like dealing with people, finding out what they need—even when they don't know it—and getting the job done. There's real satisfaction in that. Before I was assigned to you, sure, my job was definitely on the ho-hum end of the spectrum. But working on this project with you has been a complete thrill."

David nodded, satisfaction filling his expression. "I'm so glad to hear you say that."

"Why?"

"Because when my contract's up with Stockton, I want you to come work with me."

On autopilot, Cassie stuffed her purse in her desk drawer and slammed it shut. For long minutes, all she could do was stare at her monitor and the screen saver of swimming fish and the occasional flippered toaster. Every once in a while, an alien spaceship with the bumper sticker *Only HOT Men Are From Mars* zipped across the screen in a trail of bubbles.

Work with David. Permanently. The prospect was both exciting and terrifying, and each sensation had one thing in common: David. Leaving Stockton for the chance of a challenging and satisfying career with David and his consulting projects was the exciting part; working with him every day was the terrifying part. It would be pure torture, considering how he made her feel.

True, she lusted after his firm ass and gorgeous face with enough mental enthusiasm to leave her panties wet on a nightly basis, but there was more to it. He was absolutely wonderful, as a person and as a man. He was intelligent, respectful and his dry humor always made her smile. It would be easy to fall for him, if she let herself. *Bad, bad,* bad *idea to fall for a coworker.*

Accepting David's unexpected job offer would be an insane thing to do. Completely crazy.

He wanted her answer by Friday.

She wondered if she had the strength to say no.

Chapter Five

Cassie felt more down and confused than ever when she got home that night. Tangled emotions along with a typically demanding day had left her without the energy to even consider doing anything other than going to bed, despite the early hour. She forced herself to drink a glass of milk warmed in the microwave, reasoning that, if nothing else, it would settle her stomach and help her sleep. In her room, she stripped down to her panties in the dark, pulled on a soft cotton cami and slid into bed. She tried her best to shut out the turmoil of the day, clear her mind and slip into sleep.

The muffled sound of voices in the hall alerted her to Sarah's return from what she assumed was yet another date. The thought of her friend's busy love life had Cassie punching down her pillow in frustration. She rolled to her side, pulled the thick comforter over her shoulder and tucked it under her chin.

As if directed by the hand of a mischievous spirit, a ribbon of moonlight crept through the window to touch the crystal bottle on the nightstand. Cassie frowned. Drowsily, she tried to remember when she'd put the bottle there, and couldn't. She'd last seen it in the living room the night before. Chalk up one more mystery to what had been, all told, a very odd evening fueled by wine, sitcom reruns and a very overactive imagination. Leave it to her to dream of a female genie instead of a tanned body builder in a glittery loincloth. Even her subconscious wasn't getting any.

The moonlight played along the sharp angles of the cut-crystal bottle, glinting on the fanciful swoops and curves. Silver flecks of light sparkled in the fluid inside the bottle, mesmerizing Cassie's tired mind.

Her last conscious thought was of how well the flecks mirrored the mercury highlights in David's penetrating blue eyes.

The knight in the silver surcoat lifted his sword in victory. The raucous crowd roared its approval. He had been stunning from the moment he stepped onto the field, elegant and savage by turns, a master of the art of war. Physicians attended his fallen opponent, then signaled for the man's servants to help him from the churned-up mud of the tournament field. A young squire ran onto the field, leading a proud destrier as black as the knight's armor. The heavily muscled horse stepped lightly despite its massive size, head high, tail and mane streaming like banners, as perfect a specimen of equine masculinity as its master was of human.

The bulk of chain mail and armor emphasized the knight's grace as he easily mounted his horse. Straight-backed, he accepted a fresh lance from his squire. A silver-and-black triangle of fabric secured to the lance's tip snapped in the cool breeze that kept the gaming fields and surrounding spectator stands from being too stiflingly hot, but not by much. Many folk waved fans or wore floppy hats as protection from the sun. The lord's box boasted a full canopy, the roof and draperies a jeweled rainbow of extravagance. The knight set his destrier to a decorous trot and guided him to the extravagant spectators box at the edge of the field. He reined the horse to a halt and tilted his head in a bow that somehow managed to be both respectful and proud.

Lady Cassandra's breath caught in her chest. She felt a frisson of sensual interest that was entirely unexpected. Uncertain, she looked at her husband.

Lord Edward's hair and beard were as silver as the victor's colors. Weariness and pain lived in the lines of a face that had taken on the gray cast of longtime ill-health. Even so, the old lion managed, for the most part, to maintain the regal bearing that had marked him since his own days as a young and virile warrior. If she could help it, none would ever learn that their wedding night years ago remained the first and last time he had ever been able to do his duty by her as a husband behind the bed curtains. Many men would have blamed the wife for that failing, but not Edward. A good and kind man despite his fierce demeanor, he had always treated her with avuncular affection. She feared he would not survive another winter. He turned faded blue eyes on her. Despite her misgivings about this scheme, he was determined. She could not refuse his most dearly held wish, and he knew it.

Gravely, he patted her arm and nodded for her to do her duty as chatelaine.

Lady Cassandra rose and approached the railing. She tried to make out the knight's features, but he was well concealed by his armor, mail and silk trappings. His helmet covered all but a strip along his eyes, which were lost in shadows. Striving to hide her nerves, she clasped her hands at her waist and forced a restrained smile. In a clear, carrying voice, she announced, "Sir David of Micheline, victory is yours."

The onlookers, noble and peasant, shouted and hooted their approbation. His martial prowess had provided them with much entertainment.

"Indeed, my lady." The deep rumble of Sir David's voice stirred a curious sensation in her belly.

"As champion of these games, you have won the right to my token."

On cue, Lady Jane glided to Cassandra's elbow. The attendant's full lips tilted in a secretive smile as she proffered a leather purse and a simple but pretty wreath composed of flowers intertwined with one of Cassandra's scarves. When Cassandra took them, the other woman curtsied gracefully and returned to her position behind the lord and lady's high-backed chairs. Holding up the wreath for all to see, Cassandra leaned forward. Obligingly, the knight tipped his lance to her. The flowers slid down the shaft to rest against his gauntlet-clad fingers.

"And the prize," she said, holding up the purse. Bulging with coins, the purse jangled musically as she tossed it lightly toward him. He caught the purse easily in one fist, tucked it into his belt.

"To fight for my lady's honor is the only prize I wish," he said quietly, so quietly she thought he spoke for her ears alone. Her heart hammered against her chest. He dipped his chin once more in a bow. When he spoke again, addressing her husband, his voice rang out. "My lord, I humbly thank you for the amusements you have offered this day. All who took the field were worthy knights. It was my honor to test their skills, and my own." More softly, he added, "Until anon, my lady."

The knight spun his destrier on its heels in a showy flash of hooves, drawing more cheers from the spectators, and sent it cantering from the field.

Her gaze followed the silver knight long after he had disappeared from view into the town of tents occupied by the tournament's contestants.

Spectators, still boisterous in their enjoyment of the day, began to leave the stands in favor of the booths and tables set up in the bailey, where the entertainment would continue with puppet shows and plays, roving musicians and dancing, and plenty of good food and drink. The nobles and commoners of higher status would join the lord and lady inside the keep, where Lady Cassandra had arranged for mummers and jongleurs to carry the revelry well into the night.

She turned to see Lord Edward, gnarled hands gripping the carven arms of his heavy oak chair, push to his feet. The grimace of pain was fleeting, but she noted it. Sitting for long periods aggravated his back, sometimes bringing on excruciating spasms that put him abed for days, but he stubbornly resisted showing his people any sign of weakness. He even refused to allow her to put embroidered cushions on the chair, seeing it as a concession to his age rather than his due as lord. She decided she would prepare a tonic for him and insist he rest in his chambers for a little while before the feasting and dancing began.

"My lady?" Jane, hands folded demurely at her waist, waited for instructions.

"Jane, please go ahead to the keep and ensure all is in order. I will join you shortly."

"At once, my lady." Jane herded Cassandra's remaining ladies from the box and started them back toward the keep.

Instructing his man to see to the noble guests who would have waited to accompany the lord and lady, Edward joined Cassandra at the railing. When they were alone, he offered his wife his arm, clasping her hand warmly when she settled it in the crook of his elbow.

"Are you certain this is what you wish, my lord?" she asked, watching his lined face for any sign of distress. She was very fond of her elderly husband. Like Cassandra, neither of Edward's two previous wives had quickened with child. The accepted belief, and the stance of the church, was that all three women were barren, that it was God's will they had not borne their lord any children. Edward, however, had a different notion, which was why he had conceived his outrageous plan.

"Very certain, my dear. That is the whole point of this tournament," he reminded her. "I want only the best for my wife. For our son."

"And if the child is a daughter?"

"Then I shall be well content if my heir is as lovely and sweet as her mother."

She bowed her head obediently. "Then it shall be as you say, husband."

As she made her steps small and slow, so Edward would do the same, she couldn't help thinking of the masterful silver knight, power and virility infusing his every motion in the day's contests. A shiver of anticipation moved through her. It was her duty to provide her husband with a child. But she accepted it could be her pleasure, as well.

"Enter!"

At the brusque command, Cassandra pushed open the door to the castle's finest guestchamber. A fire crackled in the oversized hearth. Thick rugs warmed the cold stone floor. Rich draperies hung from the bedframe, and a massive fur throw covered the wide mattress. Several platters of food waited on a sturdy table, along with pitchers of wine and ale.

Below, Lady Jane had events well in hand. The sound of boisterous laughter and high-spirited music wound through the corridors and passages. Lord Edward, ensconced in his chair at the high table, would be giving Cassandra's excuses, explaining that his dear wife would not be joining them. Overset from the excitement of the day, she rested in her rooms, and prayed all would enjoy the evening's largesse.

Near the hearth, Sir David's squire halted in the midst of adding another jug of steaming water to his master's bath and stared openmouthed at Cassandra. A hooded cloak covered her from head to toe, but she knew it would be obvious she was both female and a woman of quality.

The silver knight, back to the door, sat naked in the large tub, immersed to his waist. Alerted by his squire's frozen pose, he twisted around.

Cassandra lost her breath.

He was, quite simply, the most beautiful man she had ever seen. The lush curve of a sensuous mouth saved aesthetic features from starkness. He apparently favored a clean-shaven face, but his beardless chin shared no similarity with a boy's. Blue eyes blazed brilliantly against the contrast of healthy, tanned skin, close-cropped black hair and well-shaped brows. Sweat and droplets of water tangled the dark hairs on a chest that fairly rippled with muscles, though not as much as she might have expected.

Cassandra felt his eyes caress her face through the shadows and sensed he knew her identity despite the concealing hood. A murmured command spurred the squire to put down the empty jug and hurry from the chamber. As he passed Cassandra in the doorway, he tactfully averted his eyes.

With a flash of humor, and an unwarranted twinge of jealousy, Cassandra acknowledged this likely wasn't the first time the lad had been ousted so his master could entertain a female visitor.

The door closed behind the squire and the latch fell into place with a solid click.

Cassandra walked to the hearth, circling the tub until she had an unrestricted view of the bathing warrior. The tub had been designed to support the brawny bodies of men of war, and was roomier than most. She'd noticed the silver knight's height on the tournament field. The tub was big enough that she saw he was able to stretch his legs out until just the crescents of his knees broke the water's surface.

Mutely, she watched a bead of sweat trickle down Sir David's chest, following the valley between well-formed pectoral muscles. Male nipples surrounded by soft-seeming copper disks nestled in dark, wiry chest hair she longed to touch.

She wondered what thoughts went through his mind. She couldn't tell from his calm expression. But his eyes...his eyes burned with desire.

Cassandra drew in a shaky breath.

Sir David lounged back in the wooden tub, resting his arms comfortably along the rim, and broke the silence. "Well, my lady? Don't be shy. Come closer, so we may converse."

Cassandra steeled herself. She was chatelaine of this manse. A respected wife and lady, about a special task with her husband's blessing. This was no time to act like some terrified virgin on her wedding night.

Before she could lose her nerve, she drew back her hood and unfastened the cloak.

His eyebrows lifted, but he said nothing as he took in the near-transparent shift that was all she wore beneath. Neither did he seem surprised to find the lord's wife in his chamber. The warmth of the fire heated her back as she removed the cloak. The elaborate braids that secured her long, golden brown curls to her head made her sensitive nape feel exposed and vulnerable.

Cassandra forced her legs to move, to walk with slow, composed steps until she reached the edge of the tub. Setting the cloak on a nearby stool, she said, "Allow me to help you with your bath, sir knight."

His fingers flexed on the wooden lip, but his voice remained steady as he said, "As my lady wishes."

Cassandra selected a cloth from a basket of supplies beside the stool and dipped it in a jar of soft, scented herb soap she had made with her own hands. She started with his tantalizingly wide chest. Slowly, she smoothed the cloth over his taut skin. He felt hot and hard under the thin cloth. Mesmerized, she watched the bubbles formed by her efforts glisten on his chest. He kept his arms relaxed on the rim of the tub. A thick trail of foam coasted down the muscled plane of his chest to the water's surface. Beneath the still-clear liquid she saw the shaft of his manhood, long and fully erect, twitch eagerly. She felt her pulse begin to race. He seemed to note the direction of her gaze, because his fingers tightened on the tub's wooden rim until his knuckles turned white.

Heat washed through her body. Feeling suddenly weak, she clutched the tub for balance, her ministrations forgotten. The soapy cloth plopped into the bathwater and their eyes collided, blue with green.

Without warning, he sat up, sending water splashing over the sides and onto the flagstone floor. Hard fingers clutched her waist. He lifted her up. And dropped her into the tub with him.

Cassandra squealed as water sloshed around her, drenching her shift and making the almost-transparent fabric fully see-through. Her knees settled as if by instinct on either side of his lean hips. Just as naturally, his shaft nestled between her thighs, a hot length as hard as his jousting lance.

A faint smile curved his lips. "I believe this is what we both want, my lady, no?"

Chapter Six

Sir David seized Cassandra's mouth like the conquering warrior he was. His tongue swept past the giving barriers of lips and teeth to explore as he willed. It stroked over her tongue, teasing it to respond to his touch, glided along the roof of her mouth, tickling the ridges of her palate.

Cassandra felt her nerves settling under the wash of the first true desire she'd felt in her life. All altruistic thoughts of bedding this knight because her husband wished desperately for an heir fled her mind. There was just this moment, this man, and the way his mouth and hands claimed her body.

As if they had a will of their own, her fingers pressed into his shoulders, learning the feel of firm muscle and sinew. Sir David made a sound of masculine approval and moved his lips from hers, along her cheek to her jaw. They made another slow, nerve-tingling journey down the slope of her neck to where her breasts mounded above the sopping fabric of her shift.

His breath felt hot even through the flimsy barrier. Her nipples were hard points, the pink of her areolas as obvious as rose petals under the transparent fabric. He hooked his finger in the already low bodice and dragged it down. Her breasts popped free, bouncing gently. The tips seemed to harden under his stare. He growled his approval. She watched through heavy, water-drenched lashes as his mouth poised over one upright nipple. His lips closed over it. She gasped, then cried out sharply as he began to suck, tongue rhythmically pressing the sensitive tip against the roof of his mouth.

She realized she'd begun to rock against the hard pole of his manhood when he began to pull up the sodden hem of her skirts, gathering the fabric around her waist and exposing her naked lower body. He pushed a hand between her thighs. His fingers found her aching folds, wrenching another cry from her as he touched the hidden pearl of her sex. Until now, only she had ever drawn pleasure from touching that forbidden place, and what she felt then was a pale comparison to the response he demanded from her body with his fingers and palm.

"Oh, yes," she gasped. "Oh, sir!"

He chuckled against her breast. "Call me David, sweeting."

"David," she said, willing to do anything he ordered as long as he didn't stop what he was doing.

She felt one hand push against the small of her back, urging her to arch into him. The position thrust her breasts closer to his mouth, but all she could focus on was the fingers teasing the tight bud of nerves and the ridge of the erection nestled between her thighs. She rode it eagerly, rubbing herself along its length.

"Jesu," he breathed. The profanity shocked her, but not enough to stop, especially when he continued to tug and pinch her clit as she moved over him.

She clung to him, her hands moving restlessly over his shoulders to the nape of his neck. She stroked the back of his head, reveling in the intimacy of his short, black locks tickling her fingers.

Faster and faster he urged her to move over his stiff flesh. Willingly, she followed his lead. Ever-increasing waves of pleasure lapped against her senses, then began to roll over her with the fury of a storm. She bit her lip, but couldn't stop the excited cries that escaped her throat.

"Oh, lady," he said, the words sounding harsh and sharp edged.

Her knees clenched his hips, her thighs trembling violently as she gave in completely to the pleasure. She thrust her pelvis against him, trying to get as close as possible as lightning flashed behind her closed eyelids. She cried out again, the sound seeming to fill the chamber. Through it all, he held her exactly as tight as she needed to be held, hands firmly in command of her body as she lost control.

Her nails sank into the skin of his shoulders as she struggled to find purchase for her shuddering senses. With deliberate slowness, he sank two fingers into her woman's core and pumped with sensuous skill. Sensation whipped through Cassandra's body and she surrendered with a helpless cry. Silver sparks blazed in his blue eyes as he watched her come apart in his arms.

The sound of her passion still echoed in the chamber when she slumped against him, boneless.

Sir David stood in one smooth motion, clutching Cassandra to him. His speed surprised her out of her lassitude. Air rushed from between her lips as she clutched him with arms and legs. Water sheeting off them, he stepped out of the tub. Her braids, which had somehow come unpinned, slapped wetly against the thin cloth that still covered her back. A few of David's long strides closed the remaining distance to the thick, fire-warmed animal pelt on the stone floor in front of the hearth.

The difference in temperature from the cooler air around the tub and the welcoming heat of the crackling fire made her shiver. His eyes looked black as he stared into hers, the passion and hunger and male power in them almost overwhelming.

She imagined she looked like a wanton, with the dripping shift rucked up around her hips and tucked under her breasts, pushing them up like an offering to a wild pagan god.

Somehow, she'd forgotten about the thin leather indoor slippers until this moment. They were, undoubtedly, ruined.

David loosened the grip of one wide hand on her bare bottom and let her slide down his moisture-slicked body. The hard thrust of his cock slid from between her thighs in a taunting caress, following the curve of her body out and up until it rested against her belly. It felt like a brand on her flesh, despite the sopping-wet linen of her shift that separated them. Though she'd lost herself shamelessly in his skilled embrace moments before, her cheeks heated with the realization that her lower body was left completely exposed to him.

Nibbling on her bottom lip, she chanced a glance down. As she suspected, the gown was as near to transparent as to make no difference. He, of course, was as naked as a babe, and apparently just as unbothered by it. His body inspired far-from-maternal feelings inside her. Her clit throbbed and pulsed with the aftershocks of the pleasure he'd drawn from her with just his fingers and the hot rub of his manhood.

He growled. Startled, she looked up to find his eyes fastened on where her teeth worried her bottom lip.

He released her arm—she hadn't even realized he still held her until the loss of his support made her pleasure-weakened knees wobble—and lifted his hand to her breasts. His nails, she noticed, were pared short and tidy, the fingers and palm calloused in the way of a master swordsman.

His touch was achingly gentle as he traced the slope of her breasts with his fingertip, riding up the curve of one, sliding down to her cleavage, then up over the other. Her breathing quickened and she yearned for his touch to move lower. Press harder. Oh, if he'd only touch her aching nipples again, suck them into his magical mouth.

Instead, he found the string securing the bodice and tugged it free of its holes.

The gown was too wet to give way easily. It stayed stubbornly in place, cupping her breasts.

She shifted her stance, eyes half closing as the involuntary caress of her own thighs put pressure on her needy clit.

"This will not do, my lady," he said, tweaking her nipple to draw her wandering attention.

"Si-sir?" she stuttered.

"I want all your attention on me, Cassandra. Tonight you are mine. Is that clear?"

A bit uncertain, she nodded. What he said was true, of course. He had won the right to her body when he'd vanquished all foes on the field of combat.

Besides, she *wanted* to be his tonight. She hadn't expected to find such pleasure in his embrace. Now that she had, she was greedy for more.

Just the taste he'd given her so far made her certain of the ecstasy she would find in her single night with the dark-haired warrior. All she had to do was submit.

"Yes, Sir David. I am yours. For tonight."

His smile was mostly satisfied. Yet there was something else in his expression she couldn't name.

"Do you have many such shifts?"

She frowned at the seeming non sequitur. "Shifts? Yes, of course."

"And do you have a fondness for this particular garment?"

She looked down. It was hard to recognize the elegant, naughtily embroidered shift in the wet, tangled garment clinging to her skin. "Not particularly. One shift is much the same as another; it matters little to me."

"Good." With that, he lifted his hands to the unlaced bodice, gripped the sides and yanked. The sound of rending fabric filled her ears as he methodically tore the gown and stripped her until she was as bare as he was. He even knelt briefly to slide the ruined leather slippers from her feet and toss them aside.

Reflected flames from the fire blazed in his eyes, but heat of another kind filled his deep-blue gaze. Instead of falling on her like a rutting stag, he surprised her again by taking a step away, then another.

His eyes feasted on her nakedness. Only her maids had ever seen her in such a state. Even Edward had always come to her under the cover of darkness, sliding under the blankets to share her warmth, if not the pleasures of the marriage bed. The urge to cover herself, to shield her breasts and sex flitted through Cassandra's mind. Then it was gone.

Instead of exposed, she felt worshipped.

David's cock thrust proudly from a nest of dark, curling hair. Hairs of the same shade dusted his thighs and chest, the corded muscles of his forearms and the backs of his hands. He wasn't muscle-bound, as he'd appeared in his armor, but pleasingly lean. A wide chest tapered to narrow hips. The bulge of his thighs, the muscular columns of a rigorous horseman, was blatant evidence of his physical strength, though he'd more than proved his prowess in the lists. She thought she saw the shadow of a birthmark in the hollow of his left hip, but the flickering firelight made it difficult to be certain.

Her eyes kept getting drawn to the upthrust muscle between his thighs. His cock, the tip a ruddy brown, bobbed gently with each breath he took. The skin of that bulbous knob was the only thing about him that looked the least bit soft. She ached to touch him, to learn for herself his shape and texture, to see if the intimate flesh felt as much like velvet as it appeared.

"Do you like what you see?"

"Oh, yes," she said without hesitation. "Very much."

Not that his flesh was perfect. The raised white scars of old wounds marked his skin here and there. A particularly thick band of healed flesh curled around his thigh. About the length of her hand, it twisted up at the end like a fishhook.

It obviously didn't hinder him. She never would have suspected its existence had she not seen it.

"I'm glad," he said. "I very much like what I see, as well."

He reached for her, not to pull her to him, but to touch her braids. Again, his gentleness surprised her. He unplaited her hair, combing his fingers through the loose strands and spreading it over her shoulders and back. He folded her into his arms, crushing her breasts against his chest.

"I want to taste," he said.

With easy strength, he picked her up and arranged her on the fur rug.

Cassandra's back and buttocks sank into the thick pelt. It felt decadent. Her lips curved. He kissed the edges of her mouth and her smile widened.

The sweet gesture made her heart melt.

He began to kiss his way down her body, and she forgot all about sweetness. All she could focus on was the sinful sensation of his lips scorching a trail of need down her body.

His fingers tangled in the curls at the top of her thighs. Wanting more of it, more of him, she let her legs fall open. He praised her in a deep, rumbling voice that seemed to reach inside and caress all her secret places.

His broad shoulders pushed her thighs wider as he made a place for himself between her legs.

Using his thumbs, he spread the lips of her sex. Shocked, she watched as he stilled. His features starkly beautiful, he stared up at her. Cassandra whimpered, confused but wanting. What was he doing? How could he pleasure them both from down there?

He smiled, as if reading her thoughts. Pursing his lips, he blew one warm breath across her damp secret flesh.

Instantly, her hips pulsed up, thighs and buttocks tightening as a thrill of pleasure raced from her clit to her belly and beyond.

"So responsive," he murmured, satisfaction lacing the observation. His head dipped down. Cassandra felt the hot, wet glide of something against her taut nub. A jolt of pleasure shot through her. Belatedly, she realized he'd licked her.

"Wha–?"

"Shhhh," he soothed. The sound vibrated against her sensitive flesh, sending another thrill of pleasure into her belly. He licked her again, then closed his lips and teeth around her. He began a gentle assault on her clit, alternately lashing the hard little nub with his tongue and sucking the needy flesh with long, luxurious pulls. The stubble on his cheeks felt scratchy against her inner thighs, heightening the sensation and banishing the last reserves of her shocked sensibilities. Mindlessly, Cassandra tangled her fingers in his damp locks and pulled his face to her. Seeking any way to get closer, she hooked her knees over his shoulders and restlessly rubbed her heels along his spine.

Groaning his approval, David slid his hands to her buttocks and cupped them in his wide palms. He lifted her higher and tilted her hips to his satisfaction. The intensified assault tipped her over the edge. The release rocked her to her toes as for the second time her woman's flesh clenched and released, clenched and released in convulsive joy. Her breasts felt round and full, the soft flesh quaking with the force of her gasping breaths and feminine cries. Tears slid from the corners of her squeezed-shut eyes and her hands tugged on his hair. Through it all, his tongue drove her on, by turns soothing and exciting, until her shudders turned to shivers.

As the final trembles subsided, David reared up over her. His chest heaved with the force of his ragged breaths. His lips and cheeks glistened with her juice. His eyes blazed hotter than the fire. If she had thought his manhood impressive before, she saw she hadn't allowed him enough credit. The bold staff looked larger than ever, the thick length long and proud where it hugged his belly, below it the twin spheres in their sacs tight and obvious.

Without a word, she held out her arms to him.

With a harsh oath, he fell on her. He covered her from neck to knees, muscled body cushioned against her welcoming softness. Without guidance, his cock slid into her with one thrust, hard and deep. He twisted his hips and, impossibly, sank even deeper inside her. Cassandra gasped. He did it again. Just that quickly, her pleasure flared anew. Her hands roved over his back, then down to his buttocks, reveling in the rippling play of muscles as he worked his cock in and out of her with increasing frenzy, every motion a full-body caress. The moisture of sweat and lust made their skin slip and slide together. David's nipples felt as hard as her own, scraping and teasing against her with the rocking force of his possession.

Cassandra twined her legs around his thighs and instinctively used the increased leverage to add her own thrusts to his, enthusiastically throwing her hips against his plunging loins. A sound built in his chest. His thrusts shortened, quickened. He buried his face in the curve of her throat, catching the muscle on the side of her neck in his teeth. The possessive bite, just hard enough to sting deliciously, came with a muffled shout as she felt his cock swell inside her. It began to throb and jump and she felt the gush of his release. Instantly, her own sensitized flesh throbbed in answer, catapulting her into an ecstasy she hadn't reached with his fingers and mouth alone.

She moaned and twisted in his arms. He grabbed her hips, refusing to let her move so much as a breath away. At last he sagged against her, his body exuding the air of a man totally and completely satiated.

For long moments, their hearts seemed to pound in unison, gradually slowing from their frantic pace. Despite his release, David's cock remained hard inside her. He rubbed his face against her neck and she felt his lips move in a kiss. The sweetness of it made her eyes fill with tears.

At last, he shifted to his side, leaving her between him and the fire. The flames had burned down to embers. Without a word, David got to his feet and went to the woodbox. Taking out several thick pieces, he crouched before the hearth. As he tossed in the fresh logs, using one to stoke the coals, the light of the reviving blaze limned his body. His flesh glistened from their exertions. She saw the sway of his balls between his legs, and the semi-erect length of his shaft as he turned to her. Her hand went to her belly, which felt trembly and empty, and rubbed the sensual ache she recognized as desire.

His eyes went hooded as he watched her. His fists clenched as though he imagined his own fingers rubbing her needy belly. Without rising from his crouch, he crawled toward her with feline grace, a giant cat prowling after a mate. Stretching out once more beside Cassandra, his gaze moved over her body, taking in her tousled hair, her tongue touching her upper lip, her quivering breasts and lax thighs. She felt wanton, a harlot. A woman.

With one finger, he touched the nipple at the crown of one breast. It tightened responsively, already trained to react to his caress. She moaned. He smiled.

"I wanted you the moment I saw you," he said. "I hope you are caught up on your rest, my lady, because I'm not stopping until I have my fill of you."

With that bald warning, he renewed his sensual assault. It seemed that with the edge gone from his hunger, he could play as he wished. Teasing her unmercifully, he explored every part of her with lips and tongue, masterful hands and knowing fingers. Cassandra writhed in his grasp, eager for everything he wanted to do to her.

At last he gave in to her pleas and mounted her, this time from behind, playing stallion to her mare. The slapping sound his loins made as he thrust against her buttocks drove her excitement higher, and she shamelessly rocked against him. Hands holding tight to her dangling breasts, fingers pinching and rubbing her peaked nipples, David waited until her cries reached a fever pitch before succumbing to his own release with a harsh shout. He sat back on his heels, pulling her upright, back to his chest so his hands could roam her body as his cock twitched in its final throes. His nose nuzzled the back of her neck, inhaling deeply of her scent.

Exhausted, Cassandra pressed her hands over his, fingers tracing the strong tendons, stroking up the muscled forearms dusted with dark hair and sweat. Again the fire had burned down while they played. She barely noticed the chill of the room, her complete concentration on this wonderful warrior who had with fervent skill initiated her into the world of passion.

Quietly, so quietly she almost missed his words, he whispered, "Ah, Cassie."

Cassie?

Chapter Seven

Cassie opened her eyes. Rather than a medieval chamber filled with furs and flagstone and an orgasm-inducing silver knight, she saw the familiar confines of her room. The only eyes watching her were those belonging to a small stuffed teddy bear perched on her dresser. The fluffy pink critter sported a T-shirt with the words *Favorite Aunt* scrolled across its plump little chest.

The clock told her she had ten minutes before her alarm went off. Outside the dormer window, the sky looked blue and welcoming—a pleasant change from the rain of the past few days. Warm light from the rising sun glinted on the panes and off the angles of the perfume bottle on the nightstand. Cassie slumped against her pillow, but couldn't take her eyes away from the bottle. It appeared harmless enough. So why did she think it wasn't?

Her nostrils twitched, and she thought she caught the faint tang of man and sex. That was impossible. It had been a long, long time since a man had shared this bed with her. There was no way her sheets could have picked up the scent of a man, unless...

The jangle of the phone jerked her from her reverie.

She reached for the handset of the cordless phone—and groaned as every muscle in her body seemed to cry out in protest. It felt like she'd spent the night at the gym, moving from weight machine to torturous weight machine like a health-obsessed fool going overboard on a good thing.

Raina James

The phone rang again. Cassie snatched up the receiver and pressed the button.

"Hello?"

"Cassie, honey! How are you?"

"Mom." Cassie sat up in bed and gaped when she realized she didn't have a stitch on. Scanning the room, she found her panties and cami tossed on the floor beside the bed. Had she taken them off in her sleep? How bizarre. Her eyes slid to the perfume bottle. Her dream...had something...? No. She rolled her eyes and mentally snorted at the direction of her thoughts. Impossible. The most reasonable explanation was exhaustion after a very trying couple of days at work. Of course David, who was never far from her fantasies on the most common of nights, would play a starring role in her latest erotic dream. Caught up in the incredibly vivid dream, Cassie had taken her own clothes off in her sleep. It was as simple as that.

Marshaling her attention, she tuned back in to the sound of her mother's voice. "Sorry, Mom. What was that? I'm just waking up, so I'm not quite tracking yet."

Her mother laughed. "I know mornings aren't exactly your best time, Cassie, but it's the one time I can be sure to get you."

Cassie didn't know why her mother continued to labor under the misconception that her eldest daughter was a party girl, staying out at the clubs every night until the wee hours. To believe Cassie was out tripping the light fantastic on a Tuesday night was pushing it, even for her mother. Cassie had been a homebody when she lived with her parents, and her move to the city a few years ago hadn't changed that. Her mother refused to be convinced. "That's all right, Mom. Really, I was awake, just not out of bed yet. I'm listening to you."

Her mother chattered on about Cassie's sisters and their families, related the grandchildren's latest antics, talked about the cruise that was in the works with Cassie's father and his

68

11/12/2021

Item(s) Checked Out

TITLE   At the count's bidding
BARCODE   33029099904658
DUE DATE   **12-03-21**

TITLE   The magic misfits / by
BARCODE   33029066739517
DUE DATE   **12-03-21**

TITLE   Three wicked wishes /
BARCODE   33029071065023
DUE DATE   **12-03-21**

Total Items This Session: 3

Books are just the beginning. Use your library card to access digital materials, online learning and research tools, and more.

Get started at
www.saclibrary.org/VirtualLibrary

Terminal #   205

rising blood pressure and cholesterol levels, and his stubborn refusal to revert to a totally low-salt, low-fat diet. Since it sounded like a low-fun diet to Cassie, she couldn't blame him. Her alarm clock began to buzz and she got out of bed to turn it off. Juggling the cordless handset, she slipped into her siren-red satin robe and headed for the kitchen.

"Enough about us. What's new with you, darling?"

Cassie tucked the phone between neck and chin so she could work the tap and fill the kettle with water for tea. "Not much. Well, there is one thing."

"Oh?" Anticipation colored the older woman's voice. From experience, Cassie knew what her mother wanted to hear—that her eldest child had finally met a man she was serious about. Even better if that man wouldn't mind moving to a small town, bringing the wandering Parker offspring back into the bosom of her family.

Yet another illusion doomed to be shattered. Cassie plowed ahead with forced brightness to conceal her own mixed feelings. "David offered me a job."

"David?" It took her mother a moment to switch gears, but she caught on. "You mean Mr. Michalek, the one you're working on that big project with?"

"Yes." Cassie put the kettle on the stove and turned on the burner. "The project is almost complete. David is an outside consultant, which means that when the project's done, he'll be leaving Stockton to work with his next client. I would go back to my old job in the business office. Yesterday he offered me a permanent position with him."

Her mother tried to stifle it, but Cassie heard her exhalation of disappointment. "And I guess his consulting business is based in the city?"

"Yes."

"What would you be doing for him?"

Cassie frowned as she put a couple of slices of bread in the toaster and got a mug from the cupboard. "I'm not sure. We didn't really get into that. He said I'd start as a junior consultant, which I assume means I'd be doing the same thing I am now, acting as his assistant."

"What about the woman you were replacing? His regular assistant?"

"He said she wouldn't be coming back to work for him, that she's staying home to take care of her grandson once her daughter's maternity leave ends."

"Looking after her grandchild? Well, how fortunate that she's able to help her daughter out like that." Cassie heard the unspoken, "At least she *has* a grandchild to help her daughter with." It was all about the subtext with her mother. Never mind that Cassie's sisters had already made their parents grandparents, giving them a set of twin girls and a boy between them. Their mother would never be content until all her chicks had chicks of their own.

A high-pitched whistle filled the kitchen, and Cassie took the kettle off the stove.

"Are you going to take the job?"

Cassie froze. "I don't know." Leaning her hips against the counter, she hedged, "There's a lot to consider."

"Like what? Would it mean a big pay cut? Or not enough benefits?"

"No, nothing like that. I'd get a raise, actually, and David is extremely good at what he does, so I don't doubt he can afford pretty good benefits for anyone who works for him."

"I thought you liked working with Mr. Michalek."

"I do."

"Then what's to think about? Are you worried about advancement?"

"No, no. Nothing like that. David's offer is a great opportunity." The toast popped up, but she ignored it. "It's complicated."

"How so?"

"It just is. I can't really explain it." Abruptly, the dream image of Sir David's body gleaming in the firelight as he reared, hard and ready, above Lady Cassandra flashed into her thoughts. Cassie straightened and yanked the bread out of the toaster.

"Hmmm," her mother said. "Well, that's the work side of things. What about the personal side? Are you seeing anyone special?"

"Well—"

"So you *are* seeing someone?"

This time, the image was of Sir David, naked, in a steaming wooden tub. "Sort of." The lie came out before she could stop it. She could practically feel her mother gathering herself for an excited inquisition. What the hell had she done? "Mom, can we talk about this another time? It's been great chatting, but I've really got to start getting ready for work. I have to go by the garage to pick up my car on the way in, so I need to get out the door early."

Her mother sighed. "Sure, dear. I understand. You'll keep me posted on what you decide to do about the job, won't you? And I *definitely* want to hear more about this man you've been seeing."

Cassie didn't bother to come clean with her mother. She *was* seeing David—at work. And in her dreams. Besides, not explaining would get her off the phone faster.

They said their good-byes, and Cassie clicked the button to disconnect the call. Placing the handset on the counter, she closed her eyes. She had to get a grip. Aside from David's job offer, she had to concentrate on the job she *did* have, which, in all honesty, she hadn't been doing properly for the last several days. She needed to focus on the here and now, not her brain's presentation of what David Michalek looked like naked and aroused.

Leaving her toast and tea untouched on the counter, Cassie went to shower and dress, absently fingering her neck where she could swear she felt the possessive caress of a man's lips.

"Do you think you'll have those documents ready for Legal by two?"

Cassie cleared her throat, damning the flush she felt heating her cheeks. She couldn't get that erotic dream out of her mind. Since her arrival at work that morning, a careful thirty minutes early, she and David had been closeted in his office for a series of conference calls, with barely time for a coffee break in between. Cassie was wound so tight she could scream. David could say, "Pass the pen, please," and her slit dampened like Pavlov's dog begging for a tasty morsel. It was as though his husky voice had a direct line to her pussy. "Two won't be a problem," she choked out.

Cassie sat in one of the comfortable leather chairs in the small seating area, files and piles of paper spread on the coffee table in front of her. David worked on a tablet at his desk.

Keeping her head down as she pretended to make a note on her pad of paper, she peeked at him from under her lashes. At the same moment, David looked up to stare at her intently. She bit her lip and hoped he didn't notice her gaze on him. He dropped his eyes, giving every appearance of absorption in whatever was displayed on his tablet.

He probably wondered about her answer to his job offer, but wanted to give her time to think it over before pressing her. Why else would he seem so attuned to her today?

David looked at his watch. "Almost noon. God, have we really spent the whole morning in here?"

Cassie forced what she hoped was a carefree smile. "I'm afraid so."

"Let's break for a couple of hours, then." He flicked off his tablet and slid it into its case. "I'm supposed to meet someone for lunch, otherwise I'd suggest we grab something at the deli."

"That's nice of you." Cassie gathered her notes and files into a neat pile and scooped them up. Sternly, she forced her mind away from speculating if he was supposed to meet a woman. "But I've got lunch plans with Michelle." Which consisted of grabbing something from the vending machine and eating together in the lunchroom as per their usual routine, but he didn't have to know that.

He stood with her and they walked to the door. Opening it, he suggested, "Maybe tomorrow?"

"Sure."

Still looking up at David, she didn't see the other person in the hall until she walked into her. At the impact, the other woman gasped and Cassie caught a whiff of musky perfume. She fumbled to hold on to the files, but lost the battle as the top few folders slid to the floor, dumping papers everywhere. "Oh no!" She crouched to recover the papers and, without looking up, apologized. "Are you all right? I wasn't watching where I was going. I'm so sorry."

Someone handed her a bright blue folder. David, she realized, had hunkered down on his haunches to help her. Then she noticed the expensive shoes, the heels ridiculously high for office wear, standing on a yellow folder. Her eyes tracked up long legs to an equally high hemline, then farther to meet Amber's feline smile and copper-colored eyes.

"Oh, Cassie." She laughed. "How like you to go bumbling around. David, I've hardly seen you today. Is there anything I can do to help things move along more quickly? I know what a tight deadline you're on, and I'm sure you can use...help. If you like, I can ask Rolly to free me up to lend a hand." She brushed a strand of loosely curled hair away from her forehead.

Cassie bit her tongue, along with the urge to give one slim ankle a hard yank and send Amber tumbling. It didn't take a genius to figure out Amber's insinuation, that David could use *competent* help, a category that didn't include Cassie.

"Thanks, but no. Cassie and I are right on schedule." Tucking the folders under his arm with his tablet, David rose smoothly to his feet. Hand under Cassie's elbow, he helped her up. "Are you all right?"

"Yes, fine." She looked at the folders, papers jammed in every which way. She'd have to go through each one and make sure the papers were sorted properly before locking them in her desk. "What a mess."

"No harm done." David still hadn't released her elbow. "Come on. I'll carry these to your desk for you. You still seem a bit shaky to me."

Without a backward glance at Amber, David urged Cassie down the hall, his expression hard. "She was standing there waiting for you," he said, voice grim.

"Really?" Cassie glanced over her shoulder. Amber, fury in her eyes and hands gripping the elbows of her crossed arms, stared after them. Cassie looked up at David. "But why?"

He snorted. "That's the kind of person she is. Amber's gotten along just fine on her looks, not to mention her other..." His eyes met Cassie's and he seemed to think better of whatever he was about to say. "Anyway, she's jealous of you."

"Of me? You're kidding."

His brows rose as he guided her into her cubicle and put the folders on her desk. "Why would I be? A lot of the managers and execs think very highly of you. They know you're skilled and dedicated. Why do you think you were chosen for the project?"

Cassie didn't know what to say.

David looked at his watch and cursed under his breath. "I'm really sorry, Cassie, but I've got to make it to this lunch meeting."

"I'm fine, honestly." When he still hesitated, she smiled. It cheered her that whoever he was seeing for lunch, he considered it a *meeting*. "David, go. You'll be late."

"Okay, okay. I'll shoot you a message when I get back and we can take another look at Peterson's proposal. It's a bit eleventh hour, but if his figures work out like he says, I think we've got time to make it happen." He waved and was gone.

Her smile faded. Cassie huffed out a breath, relaxing for what felt like the first time all day. She plopped down in her chair and watched the UFO zoom by on her screensaver. She let her head fall back on her neck, and slowly moved it from side to side, feeling the tense muscles pull and ease. She couldn't glance at David today without thinking about her dream. Her hot, explosive, screaming-off-the-walls erotic dream. She couldn't quite grasp all the details, but what she did remember was...mind-blowing.

It was only her guilty imagination that made it seem like David watched her with a new knowledge in his blue eyes. Definitely her imagination. What else could it be?

She was no further along in making a decision about his job offer, either. Considering last night's nocturnal escapades, accepting was probably a very bad idea. How could she continue to work so closely with him, wanting him when she couldn't have him?

Without taking the time to organize them, she stuffed the files in her bottom drawer and locked it. She'd go through them later, once she had her concentration back.

Just then, Michelle popped her head into Cassie's cubicle. "I'm starving," she said. "You ready?"

"Yup." Cassie rummaged in a bowl of odds and ends on her desk, looking for change. "Let me scrounge up some cash and I'm all yours."

"Cool." Michelle leaned against the cubicle wall, hands clasped at the small of her back. "Wait until I tell you what happened in the elevator this morning."

"Oh, yeah?"

"Oh, yeah," Michelle said, her tone freighted with innuendo. "Let's just say it involves Amber the Witch, Roland, a spilled cup of Starbucks and a call from Wife Number Two."

Mood lightening, Cassie grinned and rose to join her friend. "This should be good. Do tell."

Looping her arm through Cassie's, her expression full of devilment, Michelle said, "Oh, I will, dahling! I will."

Cassie was more than glad to forget her preoccupation with David for a while and let her friend fill her in on the latest gossip. Funny how seemingly intelligent people forgot such technological wonders as security cameras in elevators at the darndest times.

Chapter Eight

The strobing lights made it difficult to see the writhing mass of humanity on the dance floor, twisting and gyrating to the throbbing beat of the music.

The bass *thump-thump-thump* of the music throbbed with the kind of loud that reverberated deep in her bones. The short skirt of the spaghetti-strap slip dress brushed the top of Cass's thighs as she moved with the music, caught up in the joy and abandon of thinking of absolutely nothing at all and letting her body take over. A gloss of sweat sheened her skin, the air conditioning system no match for the moist heat generated by men and women moving across the floor in a primitive mating dance that could have just as easily played out in front of a fire to the beat of animal-bone sticks and a drum made out of a hollow log. *God, it's hot in here.*

Cass gave the arm of the delicious man she was dancing with a friendly pat and began to edge away. He gripped her elbows and pulled her against a lean, muscled body with one particular muscle stirring to prove his interest. He was pretty. However, the temptation to let the flirtation carry through into something more was negligible. She shook her head. He let her go with a good-natured smile and began scanning the nearby dancers for a more willing partner. His fickleness amused her.

Cass looked at her friend, who danced nearby with her own hunky partner. She didn't know Jane well, but the exotic, dark-haired woman was fun. Catching Jane's eyes, Cass mimed returning to their table for a drink. Jane waved for Cass to go ahead.

It was darker away from the dance floor. A trick of construction and the strategic positioning of speakers took the edge off the music so patrons at the tables didn't have to yell quite so loud to be heard. Two more women sat at the table, holding their spots against all encroachers. They greeted Cass with enthusiasm, and left her alone at the table to take their turn on the dance floor.

Out of the way against one wall, the table was the one they usually staked out at this club. Cass perched on one of the stools and hooked the heels of her strappy silver shoes over the metal crossbar.

She signaled the server over and ordered something cold and sweetly tart. As she waited for her drink, Cass occupied herself watching the horde of dancers. It was actually a fascinating slice of anthropology at play. Again she thought of a mating dance. The male showed his virility with smooth muscles, smoother moves and the enticing rock and thrust of pelvis and thighs. The female, in turn, used the dance to display breasts and hips to best advantage, with a curve of the lips or dip of mysterious lashes thrown into the mix.

No wonder some cultures throughout history considered dancing akin to wickedness.

Cass accepted the drink from the server, liking the handsome lines of his young face, liking even more the male appreciation in his eyes.

The small hairs on the nape of her neck lifted. Cass didn't have to watch the Leka twins enter the room to know they were there. Her body softened in feminine surrender before she caught the first glimpse of them stalking through the crowd like alpha wolves through a pack of lesser canines. The expensive cut of their suits couldn't disguise the powerful play of muscles under the finely woven fabric. They accepted greetings as they moved through the club, but didn't waver from their goal.

Cass bit her lip. Her bottom shifted on the seat of the stool. Her pulse quickened in anticipation.

Anyone who had eyes in their head could probably tell at a glance that the Leka twins were hunters and she their very willing prey.

They stopped, separated from her by the width of the small round table. They were as alike in looks as the proverbial peas in a pod, although the description was far too cute and simple for the likes of them. Dark hair waved over strong, wide brows. Identical blue eyes watched her with expressions of hunger and want. Lush lips curved into something sinfully inviting.

"So, dear Cass," David said. "Did we tempt you?"

His twin, Mitch, continued. "Have you made your decision?"

Cass wet her lips, thrilled at the way their eyes followed the glide of her tongue. "Yes." She darted a glance toward the dance floor and Jane, the lone person who knew about the decision that had consumed all of her attention. Brown eyes almost magically alight, Jane gave her an enthusiastic thumbs-up and mouthed, "Go for it."

Cass looked at the two men so patiently waiting for her to answer. "It would be my pleasure."

"Oh, ours too," David said. With a knowing smile, he helped her down from the stool.

Mitch, his touch a caress full of promise, settled a hand on her hip and brushed a kiss on the side of her neck, just below her ear. "I have no doubt."

Effortlessly, they guided her around the tables and through the crowd to a discreet door beside the bar. With scarcely a glance at the bartenders serving the masses from behind the glossy black granite countertop, David opened the door and Mitch whisked Cass up the stairs to their inner sanctum.

She couldn't remember the precise moment she'd met the sexy owners of the Stockyard, which was strange, considering how compelling they were. The Leka twins had the kind of appeal that called to everything female inside her. She'd seen the same response in other women in David and Mitch's orbit.

For some reason, they drew her unlike anyone she'd ever known. As far as their naughty proposal went... It would be the most daring thing she'd ever done, but how could she resist?

With each step up the stairs, the sinuous silk of her red dress rubbed against the tight peaks of her breasts, the hem teased the skin of her upper thighs and the coil of arousal in her belly tightened.

David closed the door, shutting out the noise of the club. Cass's heels on the private stairs clicked a loud counterpoint to the men's more muffled footfalls. Mitch's hand rested with casual possession on her hip, fingers stroking the curve with tantalizing promise. David's gaze on her back felt as tangible as his brother's more physical touch.

At the top of the stairs, Mitch opened another door and ushered her into a dimly lit room. She moved forward, but almost immediately came to a standstill at the sight of the ceiling-tall span of glass that overlooked the club. Drawn to it, she left Mitch and David to stand at the transparent wall. Thousands of people packed the room below, pressed together on the dance floor, pushed up to the bar and crowded around the tables placed at the edge of it all. The bright, multicolored club lights flashed in a silent fireworks display that alternately illuminated and shadowed the club floor.

Cass touched the glass, pressing her palm flat against the cool surface. Since she'd never been able to see inside the upstairs room from a ground-floor perspective, she assumed there was a reason for that. She glanced over her shoulder at the two men, noting that they'd closed the door.

"One-way?" she asked.

"Of course," Mitch said. Silently he and his brother joined Cass at the window, one on either side. Their body heat warmed her.

"We like to keep an eye on things, but unobtrusively," David explained.

Cass nodded.

Mitch slid his arm around Cass's waist as David ran the backs of his fingers along her upper arm and shoulder, skimming over one of the thin spaghetti straps that held up her dress.

"Does it bother you?" Mitch asked. "The idea that you can watch all these people while they haven't got a clue what we're up to?"

David leaned close. His tongue flicked the curve of her shoulder.

She was surprised to realize how titillating it was to understand that no one but the three of them knew what they were doing up here. They could do anything to each other, with each other. With her. Cass's excitement built. "Not at all."

Cass forced herself to turn away from the window. In the silent light show that filled the room, the men's eyes were shadowed. Still, they seemed tuned to her every movement. Waiting.

As casually as she could, Cass surveyed the room. A small bar, complete with ebony counter and high stools to match the décor of the club below, took up part of the wall opposite the windows. In between, a large seating area of couches and chairs gave the impression of expense and comfort. The furniture was obviously built to suit the proportions of the men who were the masters of this place. The seats were wide, the height made for longer legs and masculine frames, the colors dark and elegant. She didn't miss the large flat screen mounted on the wall at a right angle to the bar, nor the arrangement of a complicated-looking sound system and multimedia center.

A few hallways flowed away from the main room. She assumed they led to bedrooms, offices and a bathroom or two. It was, all in all, a masculine suite that suited the Leka twins perfectly.

For the benefit of her audience, Cass put a little extra sway in her hips as she walked to the couch parallel to the wall-wide window. She sank into the cushions. Thankfully, an underlying firmness stopped her from sinking too far and ending up in an undignified sprawl in her tiny dress. She crossed her legs at the ankles, tipped her closed knees to the side in a ladylike pose, and folded her hands on her lap.

The club lights shining through the windows put the men's strong forms in silhouette. She could almost feel the sexual tension rolling from them as they waited for her to take charge, to take the first step in this primal dance. The power was almost as heady as her arousal.

"Well, gentlemen." Her voice had taken on a husky note of lust she didn't bother to hide. "I believe you said something about needing a judge to decide which man is the better lover. I'm the woman for you. Let's start with the easy part... Strip."

There was something empowering about watching two men respond to her commands as she waited for them to pleasure her, more so as she waited like a queen, clothed and untouched. Knowing they would be doing their utmost to outperform each other tonight was enough to make her breathless, and they'd barely begun.

Mitch and David stalked away from the window to stand before her, almost close enough to touch. The glow from the small spotlights above the bar chased the shadows from their features, highlighting the planes and angles that made them, in her eyes, matching visions of male perfection. Their pure masculinity made the pretty features of her dance partner from earlier and the young face of her server seem like so much fluff without substance. Watching her from identical eyes gone brilliantly blue with passion, they began to take off their clothes.

Without an ounce of hesitation, Mitch reached for the black tie at his throat and slowly dragged the knot down.

David, with an equal air of confidence, unbuttoned his suit coat and shrugged it off, tossing it carelessly onto a nearby chair.

The ends of his tie dangling, Mitch began to unbutton the tailored gray shirt that matched the flecks of silver in the twins' blue eyes.

David, more impatient than his brother, loosened his tie and unbuttoned his cuffs and the top fastening of his shirt. Then, with a ripple of chest muscles that made Cass's breath catch in her throat, he pulled the lot off over his head and threw the clothes over to join his jacket.

"Show off," Mitch muttered. In seconds, he had carelessly tossed jacket, shirt and tie on the chair with his brother's garments.

It was easy to imagine them on a stage in front of hundreds of screaming women as they took their clothes off to something raunchy and wild.

But, no. She didn't want to think things like that. Tonight, they were all hers.

Bare-chested, they were magnificent. Their slacks hung low on their hips, and she saw faint shadows in the toned hollows beside the upper curve of their hipbones. Black hair curled on their chests in a near-perfect T, not too much, just enough to emphasize the sculpted musculature that made her fingers itch to touch. The T trailed down to circle the small indentations of their navels, the dusting of hair flaring slightly before disappearing behind their waistbands. She saw, too, the hard thrust of their aroused cocks, barely contained by the fabric of their pants.

Cass made a sound in her throat, a cross between a purr and a moan. They stilled. Something in her expression must have tipped them off to her appreciation. Mitch's chest rose with a deep, indrawn breath. The defined muscles of David's belly twitched and his cock seemed to swell behind his zipper.

In unison, Mitch and David reached for their belt buckles. Cass held her breath as long, strong fingers worked leather through buckles, unbuttoned and unzipped without fanfare or embarrassment. Pausing just long enough to toe off expensive shoes that had surely never before been treated so carelessly, they whipped pants and underwear down the muscular columns of their thighs and kicked their clothes aside. Freed, their cocks thrust impatiently out from their bodies.

Cass's clasped hands clutched each other as she controlled the impulse to reach for the men's cocks, to touch, to hold, to learn the feel of them. Her heart raced and her pussy felt wet and wanting, but she took the time to study the men.

The thrust of Mitch's cock tilted ever so slightly to the right, bobbing noticeably with the throb of his pulse in the thick vein that ran the length of his erection. A pearly drop of liquid beaded on the plum-shaped head. Blood flushed the skin of his cock a ruddy red distinctly different from the warm-brown, all-over tan that covered him head to toe with the barest trace of a paler line at his waist and the tops of his thighs.

David was every bit as mouthwatering as his brother. Here, she finally found evidence that these were two different men, not just a carbon copy of one fine specimen. David's cock tipped proudly to the left. Where his twin's skin was unblemished, a hook-shaped white scar the length of Cass's hand slashed down the top of David's thigh. It obviously had once been a very serious wound, though it looked like an old one. He'd never limped that she'd noticed. Cass frowned. Blemish was the wrong word. It was thrilling to know he'd conquered such a devastating injury. She found the evidence of his mortality a turn-on, proof of his virility and power.

As she stared, David's cock jumped. He widened his stance and between his legs she noted the heavy round orbs of his balls in their velvet sac.

Mitch's hand went to his own cock, drawing her attention away from his twin. Fisting it, he tugged his hand to the end in a slow glide. Moisture glistened on the bulb of his erection. Eyes heavy lidded, he dragged his thumb over the tip, smearing the fluid around. Captivated, she watched as his fist pulled back up the thick length and made the return trip. Cass's breath hitched and she pressed her clasped hands harder into her lap.

"Cass," David said. He had to repeat her name before she could tear her eyes from Mitch's teasing strokes.

"Hmmm?"

Now that he had her attention, he cupped his balls in the palm of his hand. He rolled them through his fingers, tugging on them with such force she would have thought it painful if it weren't obvious how much he enjoyed the roughness. His cock twitched and jumped, and liquid oozed from the tip.

The sight of these glorious men fisting themselves was the most erotic thing she'd ever seen.

"What would you like us to do next?" Mitch asked, his voice tight with restrained passion. "Much as I love the sight of you eating us with your eyes, I'd rather touch you instead of myself. David?"

"Oh, definitely." David's hand stilled, clamping tightly just behind the head of his cock. He sucked in a breath. "Love, let us have you. How can you make your choice if we don't?"

Cass weighed the pleasure of watching them continue to stroke and pull and tease themselves until they spurted over their own hands versus any stroking and pulling and teasing they might do to her. And she to them.

"That's what I'm here for, lovers."

David groaned. Mitch hissed an irreverent prayer under his breath. Then they fell on her.

Chapter Nine

Mitch crouched at Cass's feet and reached for her. Strong palms cupped her knees, slid to her ankles and untangled them, then moved back up to spread her knees wide. Eyes never leaving hers, his head dipped down to press a kiss on the sensitive flesh of her inner thigh, just below the hem that barely hid her wet, needy pussy.

David, not to be outdone, prowled onto the couch beside her. His weight on the cushions tipped her ever so slightly toward him, enough that when she tore her gaze from Mitch's hot eyes to look at his brother, David's lips caught hers without effort. The kiss sizzled. His tongue glided along the seam of her lips. She parted them in helpless invitation. He continued to tease and taste them. When his tongue finally slid in to meet hers, she sighed and felt an unknown tension in her shoulders ease. She was really doing this.

A nip on her inner thigh made her gasp and draw back from the kiss for just an instant. Mitch grinned wickedly. As she watched, he laved the tiny sting with his tongue. Undeterred by the distraction, David followed the line of her jaw to her left ear, where he sucked the lobe into his mouth then pressed hot kisses along the side of her neck.

Mitch's hands began a slow glide up her thighs. The hem of her dress caught on his wrists and followed them up. His palms moved around to cup her ass, lifting her slightly from the cushions. He stilled. Cass bit her lip to hold in a smile. She felt the rough rise and fall of his chest, cradled between her knees.

The pads of his fingers twitched, tracing widening circles as he explored her skin. He adjusted the angle of his wrists ever so slightly. The silky fabric of her dress fell away, exposing her lower body. His nostrils flared and the heat in his eyes turned incandescent.

"God, I thought it was my imagination. You aren't wearing panties? That is so fucking hot," he said.

On her left, David lifted his head and stared at what his brother's questing hands had revealed.

"You were out on the dance floor in this little slip of sin and nothing else?" he asked.

It was Cass's turn to give a wicked grin. She tangled her fingers in Mitch's slightly tousled hair and laid her palm against David's cheek. "Yes. Does it bother you?"

David laughed. "Not at the moment, no. Ask me again the next time we're on the dance floor." He leaned forward and took her mouth with renewed urgency.

Mitch's chest quaked with a low chuckle. His palms on her ass jerked her lower body forward on the cushion. His breath feathered over her wet, aching pussy. She'd expected it, but still bucked at the first touch of his tongue at the top of her slit. His firm grip controlled her easily. His kiss, every bit as skilled as his brother's, played over her most sensitive flesh, licking and teasing with tongue and teeth.

Not to be outdone, David's fingers slid into the loose brown curls at the nape of her neck and tilted her face to his. The faintest of bristles met her touch as she continued to cradle his cheek in her palm, feeling the work and play of muscles as he concentrated on pleasing her. Satisfied with the position of her head, his hand trailed down her neck. Hooking one strip of scarlet fabric in his fingers, he eased the strap down her right shoulder. The top of the dress flowed down her skin, momentarily catching on the hard thrust of her nipple. He pulled away to stare down at her chest.

"Hell. No bra, either. You're killing me."

Held in place by just the single strap, her dress clung to her left breast. The skin of her right breast looked creamy pale, tipped by the raspberry brown of her turgid nipple.

Mitch shifted, nudging her legs wider. Before she realized what he meant to do, he let go of her ass and gripped her thighs, lifting them to drape over his shoulders. Her calves settled against the long muscles of his back. His skin felt hot and satiny against hers.

He lifted her pussy back to his lips just as David sucked her nipple deep into his mouth. The dual sensation made her cry out, almost overwhelmed.

The hot suction of Mitch's mouth made her want to scream as he caught the tight bead of her clitoris with his teeth.

Beside her, David moved to his knees. Without breaking off the sweet torture as his tongue lashed her nipple, he flicked the remaining strap off her shoulder. Cass maneuvered her arms free and the dress pooled at her waist.

With one hand, David plumped her right breast to force the ultrasensitive bud deeper into the strong suck and pull of his mouth. With the other, he shaped her left breast and pinched the equally firm nipple at its crest.

Cass let her head fall back against the couch, eyes closing as she gave herself over entirely to their ministrations.

Without conscious thought, her nails raked through Mitch's hair, urging him closer. He obliged with a growl, fingers digging into her ass as his tongue darted in and out of her cunt.

Cass began to writhe and cry out, alternately thrusting her hips toward Mitch's bowed head and her throbbing breast into David's mouth. With a hollow popping sound, he released her nipple and pulled away. Cass's eyes snapped open and she lifted her head in protest. Pinching the glistening tip between thumb and forefinger, he switched his attentions to her left breast.

A renewed burst of sensation shot through her.

Eyes narrowing, she reached for and found one lightly-haired thigh. He shivered at her touch. His mouth slackened for the span of a breath. Deliberately, she scratched her nails up his thigh, fingers tingling as they encountered the thicker, more wiry hair near his groin.

Her thoughts scattered again. It was difficult to concentrate on her goal with Mitch creating such a delicious distraction. Low in her belly, the knot of desire pulled tighter with every stroke of his tongue around her clit and inside her cunt.

Somehow his fingers had shifted until the very tips moved restlessly against the cleft of her buttocks. She felt one long finger trace the line of them, delving between until he found the tight rosebud of her anus.

David, thigh muscles taut under her halted fingers, renewed his sensual assault on her breasts and aching nipples.

Looking at the two men, heads bowed, short, dark curls reflecting the ruby, sapphire and gold flashes from the club lights beyond the window, Cass reached for a kernel of control.

Her hand closed over David's marble-hard cock.

His reflexive groan sounded as if it had been ripped from his very soul.

Deliberately, she moved her hand, dragging her palm along the shaft to squeeze the bulging corona. A spurt of hot liquid hit her palm and the sea-salt scent of come joined her own feminine musk.

His head jerked up, freeing her nipple.

"Oh, fuck," he said, and buried his face between her breasts. David's hand caught hers, holding it tight around the seeping cockhead as if to stem an impending tide.

It seemed to work, because the come welled a bit in her palm, but no more.

Then the tip of Mitch's finger breached her ass.

The sting of pain, combined with the earthy smell of David's near-release sent Cass over the edge.

The knot of desire unraveled and her thighs clamped against Mitch's head. Heat roared through her veins, bringing with it a scorching wave of release.

David again took her left nipple in his mouth, somehow matching the rhythm of his suckling to the pull of Mitch's mouth between her thighs. The two men worked in stunning concert, drawing out her orgasm until repletion washed through her and she sagged into the cushions, heart pounding, quivering breasts rising and falling as she gasped for breath.

Still a little stunned by the power of her release, Cass realized her legs had clenched so tightly around Mitch's kneeling form that her heels had to be digging into his back. He didn't seem to mind. His cheek rested against her inner thigh. As her breathing steadied, his face moved in an intimate caress that rasped the hint of beard on his cheek against her skin. She must have let go of David's cock, because her fingers clenched his hip as he nuzzled his way up her throat to take her lips in a slow, luxurious kiss that made her purr. He pulled away. She sighed and gave David a dreamy smile.

"Not a bad start," he said, surprising a laugh out of her.

"No," she said. "Not bad at all."

Mitch pushed up from his kneeling position and sat on Cass's other side.

"Hey brother, stop crowding the lady," he said.

David ran the backs of his fingers down the line of her left breast. "I think the lady likes being crowded."

"Hmmm. Well, I can't argue with you there," Cass agreed.

"Let's try another tack then," Mitch said. He took her chin in his hand and tilted her face to his. "My turn," he said on a husky whisper.

Mitch quickly proved he had just as much skill as his twin when it came to firing up her hormones—as if she'd had any doubt.

The taste of herself on his lips and tongue momentarily distracted her. Like David, Mitch seemed to be the kind of man who didn't mind sinking into a deep, steamy, tickle-your-nerve-endings kiss. Cass reached a hand up to trace the curve of his jaw. He made a sound deep in his chest and settled closer against her right side. His cock felt hard and silky smooth against her waist. His hand lightly stroked her right nipple. The bud, still hard and sensitive from her orgasm, responded instantly. She squirmed in sensual delight as the twin on her other side slid his hand between her thighs and began to play in the slick flesh of her pussy. He flicked the nodule of her clit with one nail. Mitch swallowed her gasp, then eased away.

When she thought David might move away too, she grasped his wrist and held his hand in place between her legs. He nibbled her earlobe and laughed softly, but she got what she wanted. His fingers resumed their play.

"Cass?"

She turned her head toward the sound of Mitch's voice and opened her eyes. "Hmm?"

"Do you want to stop?"

She blinked. "Excuse me?"

"Do you," David pressed a kiss on her shoulder, "want to," his lips moved to the edge of her mouth, where his tongue flicked out in a teasing touch, "stop?"

"God, no. Whatever gave you that idea?"

Both men gave her equally smug smiles of male satisfaction. "Just checking, sweetheart," Mitch said. "We don't want you to do anything you don't want to."

Cass wanted to roll her eyes. Did these two gorgeous, beautiful, irresistible men think she was some kind of superwoman? As if she could say, "Thanks for the orgasm—see you later." Hell, no. She wanted everything they had for her. Since they were so conveniently positioned, she took a hard, long cock in each hand. The men hissed at her touch and satisfaction filled her. "And leave all this?"

"Thank God," David said.

Mitch didn't bother speaking. He pulled away from her clasping hand. Standing, he scooped her into his arms with easy strength. After a wobble of surprise, Cass grinned and wrapped her arms around Mitch's neck. He started toward one hallway, David hot on his heels.

The door at the end of the short hallway opened into a large, private bedroom. The room's ceiling-high, one-way windows looked out over a slightly different angle of the club. Cassie was certain the décor was something powerful and masculine, just like the Leka twins, not that she noticed. She only had eyes for the massive king-size bed. A midnight blue spread covered the mattress, the head of it full of a dozen jewel-toned pillows.

With a playful twitch of his arms, Mitch pretended to toss her onto the bed. Cass squealed and tightened her arms around his neck.

"Twelve-year-old," David taunted his twin as he stripped off the bedspread to uncover the equally dark sheets underneath.

"I hope not," Cass said, feeling a little breathless.

Mitch settled her on the bed like he handled a porcelain doll. He picked up her foot, unfastened the strap of her shoe and let it drop to the floor. "Sweetheart, I'm no boy," he said, fingers dealing with her remaining shoe just as deftly. In one smooth motion, he peeled the hopelessly crumpled dress down her legs and added it to the shoes on the floor. He crawled onto the bed, took her into his arms and rolled her partially onto his chest. "I'm perfect for you."

Something in the way he said that, the intent expression in his eyes, made her stare at him. Before she could puzzle over it too long, he tangled his fingers in her shoulder-length hair and tugged. That was all the encouragement she needed to resume the melting kiss he'd initiated in the main room. Her knees spread until she straddled one muscular thigh.

The mattress sank behind her as David joined them on the bed. First his body heat whispered along her back, then his chest and thighs touched her.

As she kissed Mitch, her hand unerringly found his erect penis. She walked her fingers down until she could cup his heavy sac and the firm balls inside the slightly rough pouch. Without breaking the kiss, he murmured a sound of approval and shifted so she could hold more of him. Almost unconsciously, she rubbed her breasts against his lightly furred chest, delighting in the rasp of his chest hair. She used her nails to trace patterns on his scrotum, then teased his inner thighs—apparently a sensitive area, because his hips surged reflexively toward her and this time she swallowed his gasp.

David's hands slid up her torso from behind and cradled her breasts, easing her a crucial inch away from his twin. Mitch's grip had moved the hair away from her neck sufficiently

94

to bare it to David's talented lips. A shiver rolled down her spine as he nibbled the nape of her neck, all the while squeezing and teasing her breasts. He pinched her nipples with the exact amount of pressure she loved. How did he know? Feeling ravenous, Cass sucked Mitch's tongue deep into her mouth and ground her ass against David's groin. His cock nestled into the valley between her buttocks as if made for it. He pumped his hips in a rocking motion, dragging the hot shaft up and down the sensitive cleft.

"Fuck, that feels good, honey," Mitch said, catching her wrist in one strong hand. He let her fingers linger around his sac, but stopped the torturously good motion. "I gotta call a halt, though. Dave?"

"On it."

With a forceful tug, David pulled Cass away from his twin. He nestled her back against his chest and his hands began to rove as Mitch left the bed. While one of David's hands continued to toy with her breasts and nipples, the other slid down her belly to the curls at the top of her thighs. He delved past them to the wet surface between her nether lips and the tight clit between them. Then he began to stroke her, hard. Cass whimpered and tried to grab hold of something to anchor her. The fingers of one hand fisted in the sheets. With the other, she reached back to clutch David's strongly muscled ass.

"Yeah," he said in her ear, his voice a rough rumble. "Hold on to me, baby."

She was helpless to do anything else, distantly aware of the sound of a drawer opening and closing, foil ripping.

Then Mitch was back, his mouth sucking strongly on the breast his twin held up for him like an offering. Without warning, David's hand moved away from her pussy and Mitch settled his hips between her legs. The way she half reclined against David's thighs and belly seemed to suit Mitch. He thrust his cock deep into her cunt, strong and sure, her inner muscles offering the smallest resistance.

Cass cried out, sounds escaping her throat with harsh abandon as he rode her with a pounding rhythm that seemed to match the headlong race of her heartbeat. The orgasm broke over her senses, tearing a scream of pleasure from her.

"Cassie, that's it, baby."

She didn't know which man spoke. It could have been either, or both. It wasn't "Cass," but she liked the way he said the feminine-sounding nickname.

Mitch rolled to his side, taking her with him. Her hips kept the pace, prolonging her orgasm. Prolonging it...hell, she might as well have been on a thrill ride without end, she thought, as the pleasure climbed up the peak again.

She definitely felt it when something pressed against her anus, something cool and damp. It nudged against her with insistent pressure without quite penetrating. She slowed the frantic thrust of her hips against Mitch's. He slowed too and ran a hand along her hip, as if in reassurance.

"Cass?" She heard the strain in David's voice as he repeated the query. "Cass?"

"Yes." Even to her own ears, the word sounded hissed, her voice drunk with pleasure. Mitch sucked the skin on her neck, near her collarbone. The thought of his love bite marking her skin thrilled her.

"Baby, d'you want me to stop?" To illustrate what he meant, David rocked his hips ever so slightly forward, nudging her anus again with the tip of what was obviously a condom and lube-covered cock.

Cass took a deep breath and tried to think. She'd never enjoyed anal sex before. She'd certainly never, ever tried double penetration. The men waited patiently, Mitch kissing her throat while David rubbed his chin over her shoulder blade. Despite the very impressive erections of both men, neither of whom had fully come so far, she knew without asking that they would accept her choice, whatever it might be. That decided her. If there was ever a man—men—she would feel comfortable experimenting sexually with, David and Mitch Leka were it.

"No," she said, looking into Mitch's blue eyes. Turning her head, she met David's matching blue gaze. "No. Don't stop."

David's lips curled at the corners. He kissed her lips. He slid the hand that held her breast out from under her and used it to brace himself against the mattress, angle his body up. Gripping her buttocks with his other hand, he gently spread one cheek. As he did, Mitch hooked her knee and drew it up over his hip, spreading her even wider. Then David began to move.

There was some discomfort, no denying it. When his cock, thicker than any finger, breached the tight hole, it hurt. But it was like nothing she had ever felt before. Behind her, David quaked with an all-over shiver. He gathered himself, an action she felt in the tensing of his thighs and belly, and eased his hips forward. He swung his hips away, then back again, nudging deeper into her rear channel with every forward thrust. Finally, his groin came flush against her ass, and she knew he was all the way inside.

"You okay?" he rasped.

"Mmmm."

"Cass," prompted Mitch, who had remained still as his twin forged into her almost virgin ass. "Are you all right, honey?"

"Yeah." She tried an experimental wiggle that made both men catch their breaths. She felt on the verge of unbearably full, with Mitch's cock in her pussy and David's in her ass. For the first time she noticed they had lost their air of suave knowledge. A mist of sweat coated their skin, highlighting their beauty as perfect male specimens. Their chests heaved with ragged breaths, and tension made their handsome faces appear stark. She could almost see the way they leashed their desire, waiting for her to accustom herself to this new delight. "In fact, I'm more than all right."

Again, she wriggled, a sinuous shift from one lover to the other. It was too much for the men. As if freed from any constraint, they exploded into action. Mitch surged forward as David pulled away; David thrust forward as Mitch fell back. Within a few strokes, they moved like they were made to do this, alternately giving and taking with such natural ease it was like they were one person instead of two.

All she had to do was hold on. Mitch and David separately were surely devastating lovers; together, they were superhuman.

Cass loved it. At this instant, she felt like she loved them.

Pleasure roared through her body. Her fingers clenched and unclenched, holding on to one man, then the other. Her legs clamped around Mitch, one calf hooked around his heavy thigh. Her breasts were crushed against his chest. Flames traveled her veins, racing to the inferno building in her lower belly. Unbelievably, she held on, held it off.

Some subtle shift in the way they moved told her they were about to go over the edge. It was enough. Cass let go with a scream, reveling as her pussy and ass clenched and milked the men's shafts in the most powerful orgasm she could ever remember. David's teeth sank with gentle ferocity into the ball of her shoulder, muffling his shout as his cock jumped inside her ass. At the same instant, Mitch yelled his satisfaction as his cock pulsed and throbbed. The three of them moved in synchronicity, the motions of each adding energy to their release until they slumped against the sheets, sweaty and spent.

For long moments, no one spoke.

"Well." Mitch, his voice gravelly, lazily stroked Cass's nipple. David, body conforming to the back of Cass's as if he had no intention of moving anytime soon, nuzzled the curve where her neck met her shoulder. "This begs the question," Mitch continued.

"What question?" she asked.

"The question of which one of us is the better lover."

Cass hid a smile, then made a production of covering a yawn as she snuggled deeper between the two men. Their cocks had softened inside her, beginning a slow retreat from her body. "Isn't it obvious?"

She didn't have to see their frowns to know they were there.

David asked, "Obvious?"

"Of course. It's me. I'm the best lover."

After a moment of surprised silence, they laughed.

Pleased, Cass gestured vaguely toward the foot of the bed. "Could one of you big strong men grab the spread, please?

"But maybe we need to work harder to convince you," Mitch said.

As tantalizing as the offer was, sleep was fast becoming a priority for the sated and exhausted woman. She was so relaxed, her bones felt like it would take an army to move her.

"Sweetie."

This time, the yawn was a real one. "I really can't decide. Don't know if I ever will. It might take a long, long time. Days. Weeks. Months." She yawned again, her thoughts becoming fuzzier. "Forever," she mumbled.

"I could work with that," the familiar male voice whispered. "Count on it, Cassie."

"Hmmm?"

"Nothing. Go to sleep, sweetheart."

Warm arms gathered her close and she did just that.

Chapter Ten

Cassie moved around the table, setting a bound portfolio in front of each of the dozen Stockton executives. Returning to David's side at the head of the table, she made sure the laptop and remote were ready to run through his presentation on the wall-mounted SMART board.

It had been a grueling day. The meetings, including this final one with the most senior executives in the company, had consisted of an overview of the major steps in the transition, what had been accomplished, and the few tasks that remained to be completed. While nothing in the presentation had been unexpected, the executives still had a surprising number of questions, sometimes about the most inconsequential of items. David handled it all with a calm aplomb Cassie admired. She wished she could be half so patient with the pure repetitiveness of it all. Didn't anyone ever read reports or check their e-mail? Even if David didn't seem to mind, she was exasperated on his behalf.

Cassie returned to her chair against the wall, within easy reach if David needed anything. She wasn't alone. Each executive had arrived at the meeting with his or her assistant in tow. They, too, were seated along the wall like an outer ring of servants ready to jump to the assistance of the lords and ladies. Cassie smiled at the women seated on either side of her and prepared to make note of the executives' questions and who asked what, to put into yet another report to be distributed later.

David clicked the remote to bring up the opening screen of the presentation.

"Hold on, David." Roland held out one hand in a staying gesture, eyes on the report he'd just flipped open. "How long do you anticipate this will take?"

"Forty-five minutes for the presentation itself, not including any questions that arise during or after."

Roland turned to the woman seated behind him. "Amber, could you order us up some dinner? Have the coffee shop down the street send over something. Sandwiches and whatnot, along with some carafes of coffee. You know what I like." He looked at the vice presidents and directors seated around the table. "No offense, but I can't stand the stuff we stock here."

Some smiled, others chuckled in agreement.

Amber gave a professional smile and stood up, leaving her notepad and pen on the seat of her chair. "Of course, Mr. Roland."

So much for "Rolly". Cassie thought Amber's smile looked just the teeniest bit brittle. She imagined Amber didn't enjoy being called on to do the menial executive assistant tasks that were her job, while the other EAs got to listen in on the meeting in its entirety.

Dinner plans taken care of, David started the presentation. As the sessions had throughout the day, it went smoothly. It involved a broader overview than the information tailored to each previous group. David had to pause several times for questions and again when Amber rolled in a cart with the sandwiches and coffee.

Cassie would have forgone juggling a napkin on her knee, but David stalled that plan. Saying he knew she'd barely had time to stop for lunch, he stared her down until she stood and accompanied him to the spread of sandwiches and finger food arranged on the sideboard. While she ate, he poured her a coffee and competently doctored it just the way she liked it. She wondered when he'd noticed she preferred three sweeteners and just a small splash of cream. The crooked smile he gave her with the cup made her heartbeat trip a little. She felt her cheeks warm.

"Almost done," he said, his voice low.

Cassie made a sound of agreement and sipped her coffee. "It's going well, I think."

His voice dropped even lower and he leaned his head down a few inches to say softly, "I think Richardson's lucky his EA is so damn efficient. He wouldn't know the time of day if he didn't have that woman here to check his watch for him. I swear she knows the material better than I do."

Cassie muffled a laugh with her hand, trying not to choke on her sip of coffee. She liked the fact he felt comfortable enough with her to share his dry comments, especially since she knew very well how circumspect he was with everyone else. His observation about Richardson was dead on. The man's EA, a middle-aged woman with an enviable sense of style, was a saint who deserved to earn twice what he was paying her.

"Sure you don't want to offer her a job instead?" Cassie held her breath, silently berating herself as the teasing light left David's eyes. *Why* had she asked that? She didn't know what her answer to his job offer would be—well, she knew what it *should* be—but that didn't mean she had to toss another potential candidate in his face. The last thing she wanted was for him to think she wasn't taking his offer seriously.

"I'm sure."

His low, confident tone drew her chin up and she felt her lips curving in response. "Okay, then."

David looked at his watch, then at the men and women gradually reconvening around the table. "Guess we'd better get this show back on the road."

"Right."

David returned to his seat, but remained standing as the VP of International Sales stopped him with a question about a squash date.

Almost against her will, Cassie felt her eyes flick down David's body. He was one of those men who looked really, really good in a suit. The kind of good that made a woman want to take him *out* of that suit. The tailored cut fit his body to perfection, emphasizing the width of his shoulders and the leanness of his waist. The hem of his jacket wasn't quite long enough to hide the high curves of his buttocks covered in the rich cloth of his trousers. She clasped her hands, trying to quell the overeager imagination that made her palms tingle with the need to cup those round rear cheeks.

If her dreams were anything to go by, they fit her hands like they were made to be grabbed while he pounded into her wet, willing body...

A tickle on the back of her neck jerked her out of the pleasant, and wholly inappropriate, fantasy. The sensation that she was being watched was strong enough to make her eyes dart guiltily around the room. She saw that Amber's narrowed gaze was riveted on her. Of course.

Cassie didn't know if David was right, if the source of Amber's animosity really was rooted in professional jealousy. Their mutual dislike seemed to have started the moment they met. Cassie really couldn't stand people, men or women, who thought they were too good to earn their way through life. Worse, Amber made no secret of her opinion that she deserved a much higher position than she had, or of her willingness to dig her stiletto heels into the back of anyone who got in the way of her achieving it.

Ignoring the other woman, Cassie dumped her used napkin in a trash bin and resumed her seat as David called the meeting back to order.

Due to a flurry of questions at the end of David's presentation, it was another hour before the briefing drew to a close.

Cassie quietly took care of packing away the laptop and presentation equipment while David wrapped up by asking the executives to refer to a certain section of the portfolio she'd prepared.

"I need to get together with some of our people in the Chicago office, as well as one of the vendors, to iron out the outstanding issue on page one-thirty-eight, subsection F," David said.

Roland nodded. "Fair enough. When do you expect to go to Chicago?"

"Not this weekend. I've got plans that can't be changed. Cassie, can you see what's available Monday morning? Preferably early, so we can make the most of the day. We may be able to fly home that night, but better plan on staying over."

"Monday, right." She put down the compact case holding the projector and reached for her notepad. "Wait a minute. We?"

"I could really use you with me. I hope that won't be a problem."

"Of course she'll go," Roland said.

David nodded at the CEO, but looked to her for confirmation. "Cassie?"

"That's fine. I can make it, no problem." She tried to remember if the wrinkle-resistant business suit she'd worn on the few training trips she'd taken was hanging in her closet or if it was in the bag of clothes set aside for the dry cleaners.

"Excellent," David said.

The meeting broke up fairly quickly after that, with a couple of men from Marketing and the female head of Technological Development lingering to talk to David. Roland clapped him on the shoulder with paternal friendliness. "I'll be out of the office tomorrow. Golf game with those fellows from Intersect—you know the ones, Dave—so I won't see you until you get back from Chicago. Shoot me an e-mail and let me know how it goes, all right?"

Cassie crouched down to stow the SMART board's keyboard in one of the cupboards under the sideboard.

"Of course. Good luck on the links."

Roland chuckled, as if no luck was needed. As soon as they were gone, David came to offer Cassie a hand up.

"Want to grab a bite to eat?" he asked.

Pleasure bloomed in her chest. "I'd lo–" Cassie grimaced as she remembered her schedule. "I'd love to, but I've got plans." She checked the thin gold-toned watch on her wrist. "I'm supposed to meet Michelle for drinks, and she's probably already at the club."

David smiled easily. "No problem. Another time, then."

Scooping up her files so all she had to carry was her notepad, he held the boardroom door open. As she passed him, she inhaled the faint, woodsy scent of his cologne. Then she realized that this was the first time he'd asked her to do something totally outside of work hours. Almost like a date. Something warm curled in her chest, but she quashed it and told herself to get back to reality. *It's not like he's asking me* out *out. He's just being his usual, considerate self. He doesn't mean anything by it. Exhibit A: He doesn't seem the least bit disappointed that I turned him down.* Stoically, she reminded herself—again—of her no-dating-coworkers policy. Even she thought she was starting to sound like a broken record.

To cover what her nerves told her was an awkward silence, she hurriedly said, "Before I forget, Legal sent the documents back down."

"Perfect. I'll go over them one more time tomorrow, then we can leave them for Rolly's signature on Monday."

Cassie turned into her cubicle and her step faltered. Her sudden halt must have caught David by surprise because his chest brushed her back and his hand settled briefly on her hip. "Sorry. Didn't mean to mow you down."

She flashed him a distracted smile, but her thoughts were on the whiff of perfume that had put her on the alert. Rich, expensive, overly musky—nothing she'd ever worn, that was for certain. She did, however, know someone who wore a perfume that smelled exactly like that. Amber must have just been here for the scent to be so strong.

"Something wrong?"

"No." What could she say? *David, the mean girl was in my personal space, looking at my stuff. Wah wah wah.* Not likely. "It's fine. Here, let me put those away and I'll get the package from Legal."

She took the stack of folders and set them on the shelf where she kept current, nonsensitive business, then unlocked the drawer where she'd tucked the thick brown envelope from Legal. It wasn't there. Shooting David a confident smile, she said, "I must have stuck it in a different drawer."

"No problem."

After another five minutes of fruitless searching, Cassie was steaming mad and trying not to show it. She *knew* Amber had done something with the file. She just couldn't prove it, especially if she couldn't find the file. How had the witch even known the file was in her locked drawer? And how'd she get into it? She was probably laughing her ass off, knowing how crazy Cassie would go trying to find the important package. It was just icing on the cake that David was here to see Cassie so flustered and disorganized. Imagining herself planting a fist in Amber's pretty, slightly upturned nose didn't do much to calm her.

A strong hand settled on her shoulder and gently tugged her away from the mess she was making of the files in one of her standing cabinets. "Tomorrow's fine, Cassie. You've had a long day. Take off, have your drinks with your friend. All right?"

She sighed, realizing what a scatterbrain she must appear to be. "Okay. If you're sure."

He squeezed her shoulder. "I'll see you later."

"Later," she agreed.

As he walked away, the thought of toiling away at Stockton after the project ended and he was gone made her heart ache. Sure, she had friends she enjoyed seeing every day, but they weren't David. And then there was Amber the Witch and all the stupid, petty office politics she'd be embroiled in once she returned to her old job. David's offer to leave it all behind and join his company was more temptation than he knew, completely aside from her infatuation with him.

Cassie reached for her coat, but in her distraction only succeeded in knocking it off the hook. The black trench coat slithered to the floor between her desk and the cloth-covered cubicle wall. Huffing in annoyance, Cassie stooped to fish it out. It caught on something. She tugged harder. She heard a tearing sound and the resistance abruptly gave. Off-balance, Cassie rocked back on her heels and sat down, hard.

"Oof!"

She knew she was alone, but Cassie shot an embarrassed glance over her shoulder. It would be just her luck for David or someone else to be standing there to witness it when she landed on her ass, legs splayed, skirt rucked up high on her thighs and hair falling in her face. Fortunately—and about damn time— luck was with her, and no one had witnessed her undignified tumble. Sadly she held her new coat up and examined the torn cuff. It must have caught on a hidden nail or screw. She shouldn't have yanked on it so hard. Then her eyes caught sight of something else.

The slim edge of a brown envelope.

Cassie scrambled to her knees and shoved her hand into the dark space between her desk and the wall. It was, of course, the envelope from Legal. Amber must have hidden it there. Cassie would never have found it if her coat hadn't fallen off the hook. She would have looked like an idiot, not to mention incompetent, tomorrow when she had to tell David the envelope was gone and she'd have to get Legal to print off another copy. It was generally a bad idea to have sensitive legal documents go missing. It was the kind of thing people could be suspended for, at the very least. Amber would know that. Cassie's anger flared anew.

She really, really, *really* despised that woman.

Rather than put the documents back in the drawer, she tucked them in her satchel. Better to break protocol by bringing them home than risk Amber jimmying the lock. She'd just have to arrive extra early in the morning and hand the envelope directly to David.

Michelle was waiting. Cassie grabbed her coat and purse and strode out of her cubicle. What she needed most right now was a sympathetic ear and a drink. A strong one. Or three.

Chapter Eleven

"Where have you been?"

Cassie dropped her bag over the corner of the ladder-back stool and shrugged off her coat. "God, don't ask," she said, eyeing the fishbowl-sized margarita Michelle cradled in her small hands. Like the younger woman, she raised her voice to be heard over the sound of the energetic band playing classic rock on the club's small stage. "*Please* tell me you ordered one for me."

As the words left her mouth, a grinning waiter leaned around Cassie to flip down a coaster with all the flash of an Atlantic City blackjack dealer. He set a salt-rimmed margarita glass on the coaster and produced a small dish of roasted soybeans with a flourish.

Cassie seized the glass. "Thanks, Rick. You're a prince."

His grin was a blend of boyish charm and manly sex appeal that made Cassie briefly wish she went for younger men. In some ways, it would be simpler than pondering the impossibility of a relationship with the man she really wanted. She pegged Rick at a very tempting twenty-two. Simpler, but that kind of relationship came with its own set of problems.

"Anytime, doll," he said, oblivious of her speculations about his potential as a no-strings hookup. "Michelle told me to have it ready as soon as you walked in the door."

"Then you, m'dear, are a princess."

Michelle winked and popped a soybean in her mouth. "What are friends for?"

Cassie lifted her glass in a toast and took a long, deep gulp of the tangy drink—and gasped as the extra jolt of alcohol hit the back of her tongue. "Whoa! That's got some kick! Absolutely perfect. But how'd you know I'd need it?"

"Ah, well..." Michelle looked helplessly at Rick. Since he had smarts to go with his sexy smile, he leapt into the conversational breach.

"Can I get you ladies anything else?"

"The appetizer platter?" Michelle looked at Cassie, but didn't wait for agreement before hurrying on. "Yeah, the appetizer platter. And the dessert platter."

Rick gave a silent whistle. "Wow, the big guns. You got it."

As he walked away, Cassie stared at her friend with raised eyebrows.

"First the high-octane margarita, now the appetizer platter *and* the dessert platter? For just the two of us?" She narrowed her eyes. "All right, Sharpe, spill. What's going on?"

Michelle worried her lip with her teeth. Cassie continued to stare. Michelle relented with a *whoosh* of held breath. "Okay. All right, I'll talk. But please don't kill the messenger."

Cassie felt a sinking sensation in her stomach. Straightening in her chair, she carefully set her margarita aside and folded her hands on the table in front of her. In a deliberately calm tone, she said, "I promise I *will* kill you if you don't start talking. You're giving me the heebie-jeebies as it is."

Michelle took a long swig of her own drink before blurting, "It's Amber."

Deliberately, Cassie loosened the white-knuckled tangle that had been her folded hands. "I should have known. I guess it was too much to hope that messing with my files was all she was up to."

Michelle frowned. "Files? What files?"

Cassie pointed at her. "Uh-uh. No side trips. I'll tell you all about it after you tell me whatever has you looking for the nearest exit. Enough stalling."

"Geez. Fine. You're right." Michelle took a deep breath. The words came spilling out, as if saying them faster would make the medicine go down more easily. "Amber's been telling everyone that you're sleeping with David to get him to offer you a job with his company, and that you've been doing the nasty in every supply closet from the basement to the roof, and anywhere else you can hike your skirt, and that she caught you taking *dictation*," here Michelle paused to include air quotes, "from Little David and..."

The speedy monologue tapered off into an uncomfortable silence. Cassie's cheeks felt chilled, and she knew it must be because all the blood had drained out of her face as fury warred with mortification. What made it even worse was the fact Michelle almost shouted her report to be heard over the band's rendition of the Romantics' "What I Like About You," her obvious discomfort making her usually sweet-toned voice shrill.

Cassie slid a glance to the side. Was it her imagination, or were the people at the next table trying overly hard *not* to look at her? At least she didn't recognize any of them.

"Cassie? Are you okay? You look like you're going to pass out."

She gave herself a mental shake and snorted. "Hardly. Give me a minute, here. I'm trying to convince myself that killing her would be a bad thing."

"Definitely a bad thing."

"God!" Cassie slammed the flat of her hand on the table, setting their margarita glasses wobbling. Michelle startled and a few people at nearby tables gave up on discretion and stared openly. Ignoring them, Cassie snatched up her drink and drained it. Mostly full, it took a bit of doing, but she slugged it back like a champ. The alcohol-infused slush froze her throat and sent a fleeting spike of icy pain into the middle of her forehead, but she didn't care. Resisting the urge to slam the empty glass on the table too, she gently set it on the coaster. Michelle watched like a wary animal. Cassie picked through the soybeans as if her sanity hinged on finding the perfect one. She popped it in her mouth. It had all the flavor of Styrofoam, but she grimly chewed and swallowed.

"I am a better person than this. I will not let the petty annoyances of small, simple, stupid people like Amber Pilecky bring me down." She said it like a mantra.

Michelle nodded slowly. "Right. Small, simple, stupid. Who cares? I mean, it's not like anyone would believe her."

Cassie shot her friend a skeptical look at the blatant lie. Michelle winced and shrugged. They both knew almost everyone at the office would latch on to each salacious detail that dripped from Amber the Hypocrite's lips, whether what she said was true or not. It was human nature.

"How long has this been going on?"

Michelle squirmed. "I don't know. I heard about it a few days ago, kind of by accident."

"A few *days*? And you didn't say anything?"

"Well, it was something I overheard in the ladies' room. No names were mentioned, and since I didn't hear the whole conversation, I didn't know they were talking about you and David."

Cassie dropped her forehead on her palm and groaned.

"But then today I walked in while Amber was talking to Diane Somerfield, you know, from HR? And she gave me this sly, catty smile and just kept right on talking, like she wanted me to hear what she was saying. What could I do? You were in meetings all day, and this is the first chance I've had to say anything to you."

Closing her eyes, Cassie breathed through her nose. It wasn't a pleasant feeling, hating someone you had to see almost every day. It used to bother her, the strong, immediate dislike she'd felt upon meeting Amber. Lately, not so much.

Where the hell was Rick? He needed to shake his cute tail on over here. She desperately wanted another drink. Almost to herself, she said, "I wonder how she knew about the job?"

"Job? What job?"

Cassie lifted her head and sighed. "She did get one thing right—David offered me a job."

Michelle goggled. "He did? But that's great!"

A cheer went up as the band segued neatly into the distinctive opening riffs of "Sweet Home Alabama". A collective scraping of chair legs sounded as women, some dragging protesting men, swarmed the postage-stamp-sized dance floor. Cassie spotted Rick caught in the crowd. Somehow, he made his way through the dancers, balancing a platter on each palm. Sliding the food onto the table, he didn't bother trying to speak over the noise, just scooped up their empty glasses and gestured back toward the bar. Cassie nodded emphatically. Hell, yes, she wanted another.

A hand on her wrist drew her attention back to Michelle, who leaned over the table despite the spread of munchies and sweets. "Cassie! What job?"

"A couple of days ago, David took me to lunch."

"I remember." Michelle made a keep-going gesture with her hand. "And?"

"And he asked me to come work for him when the contract's done."

"As what? His assistant?"

"No. Not exactly." Cassie made a show of dipping a fried zucchini spear in a small cup of sour cream. Fury at Amber's conniving lies ate at her belly, but she tried to ignore it. "A junior consultant."

"Whoa! No way! And you're just telling me now? Wait a minute. Why do I get the sense you're not exactly popping handsprings?"

She shrugged. "I haven't decided if I'm going to take the job or not."

"Are you nuts?"

Cassie bit the end of the zucchini stick off almost savagely. "Nope. I just think it might not be a good idea."

"For God's sake, why?"

"I don't have any experience."

Michelle scoffed. "My ass. You could run circles around some of the execs on the top floor, and you know it. Besides, David obviously thinks you can do it, and that's all that matters."

"But what if I make a fool of myself?"

"Highly doubtful. Anyway, David will be there. It's not like he's going to shove you in the deep end of the pool and expect you to be an Olympic swimmer right away."

"It's not that."

"Then what is it? I don't get it. Your dream guy offers you a dream job–"

Cassie choked on the zucchini. "Dream guy?"

"Well, yeah. You know, David? The guy you've been drooling over for the past few months?"

"I have *not* been drooling."

Michelle pinched a bite off a deep-fried cheese stick and popped it into her mouth. "Only in the nicest way, sweetie pie. Why do you think everyone is so ready to believe you're getting it on?"

"Holy hell." Cassie covered her eyes with her palms and moaned. "You mean everyone knows how I feel about him?" Then another, more horrible, thought occurred and Cassie's hands fell limply to her lap. Staring at her friend, she said, "Does *he* know?"

"I doubt it. I mean, he doesn't act weird around you or anything, does he? Come on to you, make inappropriate comments, avoid you? I'm sure he's as clueless as most men. Besides, it's not like everyone believes you're sleeping with him to get a job offer."

"I am not sleeping with David!"

"That came out wrong. What I meant was, no one believes you're anything like that sleazy climber Amber Pilecky. Actually, everyone thinks your crush is kind of sweet."

"Crush? Crush, as in I'm trapped in high school again? You're not helping here, Sharpe."

Michelle looked at her sympathetically. "I'm sorry. Maybe I shouldn't have said anything."

Cassie sighed. "No. You were right to say something. It's better that I know what's being said than be completely oblivious to the reason everyone's laughing behind my back."

"Cassie, no one's laughing at you."

"That's what it feels like. God, I hope he never hears what Amber's been spreading around."

Cassie stilled. The small hairs on the nape of her neck lifted and she felt her cheeks flush in instinctive reaction. Just one thing made her react like that. Or rather, one person. Slowly, she scanned the club. And there he was, standing at the bar.

David laughed as he took three bottles of beer from the bartender. There was no way she could hear his voice over the music and laughter and chatter, but she knew the sound so well it was like she was beside him. He passed two of the bottles to a pair of men she didn't recognize. David said something, then took a long swig from his own bottle. Even from across the room, she could see his Adam's apple bob as he swallowed. Her fingertips tingled with the force of her need to touch his skin, feel the warmth of that strong, muscular column of flesh. She clenched her hands into fists in her lap.

David and the two other men moved away from the crowded bar counter.

Michelle theatrically cleared her throat and Cassie tore her eyes away from him.

"Not drooling, huh?"

"Oh, shut up."

Before Cassie realized what Michelle planned, her friend stood up on the stool's crossbar, raising her head well above the crowd, waved and let out a whistle worthy of a ball park. "Mr. Michalek! Hey!"

Horrified, Cassie sank in her seat and grabbed Michelle's wrist, trying to yank the other woman back down. "What are you doing?"

In a singsong voice, Michelle said, "Being your best friend ever." Ignoring Cassie's insistent tugs on her wrist, she waved her free hand again. "Over here, Mr. Michalek!"

David either noticed Michelle waving or heard her surprisingly loud bellows. He looked toward their table. He smiled and gave a single wave of acknowledgment. He said something to his companions and the three of them started to make their way around the tables and dancers on an obvious course to join Cassie and Michelle.

Michelle sat down and gave Cassie a grin. "He's coming over."

"Yes. I can see that." Michelle's smug expression remained undimmed under the death-ray glare Cassie was trying to send her. "Perfect. You know, I'll get you for this."

Before she could go into detail about her retaliation, David was there.

"Cassie. Michelle. Nice to see you." He gestured at the men with him. "This is Steve and Zak."

Cassie immediately recognized the names. David had told her quite a few stories about them. The three had shared a house in college, if she remembered correctly.

Michelle flashed a charming smile. "Unless you already have a table, why don't you join us?"

Zak, a lanky blond with the tanned skin of a man who spent a lot of time outdoors, grinned. "Sounds good to me. Steve, buddy, help me round up some more chairs."

They quickly commandeered vacant stools from nearby tables. David refused with a shake of his head and remained standing. "I'm good. I think I've been in a chair too many hours today as it is." He casually put his hand on the back of Cassie's chair.

She tried to ignore the electric attraction that his very proximity sent zinging through her veins.

David had obviously been back to his apartment, because he'd changed out of his business suit into jeans and a soft, charcoal grey pullover sweater. The small V-neck of the garment left the base of his throat exposed, and she could see a few dark tendrils of chest hair along the edge of it.

She was so focused on David that she missed Rick's return with the margaritas until he spoke.

"Sorry for the wait, Cassie," he said, leaning close to speak directly in her ear. David could have been invisible for all the attention the younger man paid him. "Are you all right? You looked a bit upset earlier."

David moved his hand until his forearm rested along the back of her stool. A quick glance showed he was watching her and Rick intently, his expression unreadable. She could feel Rick's breath against her earlobe as he waited for her answer.

"I'm fine, Rick. Something happened at work and it kind of took me by surprise." She picked up the margarita glass and gave him a friendly smile. "This'll help."

"Something happened at work?" David asked.

Rick didn't even acknowledge him. "If you need anything, let me know."

"Will do."

She watched Rick walk away, wistfully thinking again how much easier a relationship with him would be, rather than pining over David Michalek.

It was David's turn to lean close to her ear. "Something happened at work?" he repeated.

The feel of his warm breath brushing her skin had a drastically more extreme effect on her. Cassie bit her bottom lip and concentrated on breathing slow and easy. She imagined telling him about the rumors Amber had been spreading and her cheeks burned. "Oh, it's really nothing," she said. "I was just...upset that I thought I'd misplaced the file from Legal that you needed. But I found it before I left the office. No worries."

"I wasn't worried."

"Good." She lifted the margarita glass to her lips.

"She was also upset about what Amber Pilecky's been saying," Michelle said.

Cassie coughed as the sweet liquid went down the wrong way. David patted her between the shoulder blades. She managed to sputter, "Michelle!"

"What's that woman been up to now?" David asked.

"Nothing," Cassie said. "It's not important."

Michelle, finally, seemed to get a clue. "She's just been saying some not very nice things. You know how she is."

David made a noncommittal sound and tipped back his beer bottle. Cassie noticed he hadn't moved his hand from her back. *Probably forgot. Nothing special in the gesture at all. Down, girl.*

The rest of the night progressed surprisingly smoothly after Cassie relaxed. Michelle seemed to enjoy flirting with both of David's friends. Steve was a lawyer, Zak an electrical engineer. A nearby booth became vacant. Zak claimed it and they moved there, where they could all sit together without crowding around the small table. Michelle sat between Zak and Steve, while Cassie and David took the facing bench seat.

Rick paused at their table to collect empty glasses and clear a denuded plate of nachos the men had ordered after polishing off the appetizer and dessert platters. "Anything for last call?"

Surprised, Cassie looked around to see that most of the other patrons had cleared out. The band had long since left the stage, the speakers turned over to the sound system behind the bar. She stared at her watch. She couldn't remember the last time she'd closed out a bar, and on a Thursday night to boot.

"God, is that the time?"

"'Fraid so," Rick said. "One last margarita?"

"Thanks, but no. Four's my limit." She looked at the others. "I should go. I've gotta get to work early or my boss will skin me."

"Is he really so bad?" David asked.

"No. He's pretty great, actually."

"Glad to hear it."

Zak slid out of the booth and handed Michelle to her feet, then waited while Steve helped her into her coat. Cassie hurriedly pulled on her own coat before David could offer to hold it for her. In her tipsy state, she knew the gentlemanly gesture might be her undoing.

The men walked them outside, where the air was moist and fresh from a cool drizzle. A loitering cab pulled up to meet them, tires splashing through the shallow puddles beside the curb. Zak opened the rear door. Steve got in and moved to the far side. With a quick wave to Cassie, Michelle slid in beside him, followed by Zak. Before closing the door, Zak winked at an open-mouthed Cassie. "Turns out she's going our way."

The door slammed with a *thunk* and the cab pulled into the light traffic and away before Cassie could say anything.

"Well, how do you like that?" she said, almost to herself.

"She'll be fine with them," David said. He raised a hand to summon another cab waiting farther down the curb. It eased ahead into a smooth stop in front of them. David opened the door. Taking her elbow, he helped her in.

"Ease over, Cassie."

Automatically, she did as he asked. She thought the driver looked vaguely familiar, but couldn't place her. Her gaze snagged on the cabbie's license and accompanying photo in the holder on the back of the seat. Jane something, a surname with a whole lot of letters. The photo was a surprisingly flattering one. Usually, official photos tended to look more like police mug shots. The woman behind the wheel looked as lovely in the flesh as she did in the photo.

Cassie dismissed the niggling sense that she knew the woman from somewhere when David got in beside her and gave the cabbie Cassie's address.

The cab pulled away and merged with the late-night traffic.

"What are you doing?" Cassie asked.

"Seeing you home."

"How'd you know my address?"

"It's in your file."

She supposed that was valid. He could have had a reason to go through her file any number of times, especially before he offered her a job with his consulting company. "How do you know I don't have my car?"

"You never bring your car in on Thursdays. Even if you did, would you really drive home after four margaritas? Those looked like they packed a wallop."

"No, of course not. Why take chances?"

"There you go, then."

"You know, you don't really have to see me home. You live just a few blocks from here, so it's not like you need to share a cab with me. I'm a big girl. I can get home all by myself."

"I know you can. But my mother raised me to be a gentleman." He paused. "Usually."

"Oh? So when aren't you a gentleman?"

His smile was slow. "Someday, I'll tell you."

A pleasant shiver rolled up Cassie's spine.

Reminding herself it would be a really, really bad idea to make a fool of herself and kiss him when he was just being friendly and fun, she looked out the window. The raindrops on the glass captured the reflections of the streetlights they passed, creating a dreamy collage comprised of hundreds of tiny candle flames. The driver's radio murmured softly in the front seat. David's thigh and shoulder pressed comfortably against hers. The scent of his spicy aftershave was easy to detect over the odor of fast food, sweat and heavy pine courtesy of the cardboard air freshener that dangled from the rearview mirror.

It wasn't hard to imagine they were going to her place after a night out together. Instead of coworkers, they were lovers. She wouldn't have to invite him up, he'd just know he was welcome. The cab would pull up in front of the old Victorian. David would get out and hand her out of the cab. They'd climb the four flights of stairs to the third floor together and...

"Have you given any more thought to my offer?"

Just like that, her pleasant fantasy evaporated. She wished he hadn't asked her that. Now she'd have to refuse, instead of just thinking about refusing, and the deed would be done. Then it would be over. David's contract would end, he'd leave the company and move on to his next project. She'd stay behind and have to face the Amber Pileckys of the world, day after day. But it would be the heart-smart thing to do. She looked at David and opened her mouth.

"Forget I asked," he said, shaking his head. He gave her a rueful smile. "I told you I'd give you time to think it over, and here I am pressuring you. Tomorrow's soon enough."

The cab rolled to a stop in front of Cassie's building. The cabbie threw it into Park and turned to face them. Even though she wore her thick, black hair pulled back in a simple ponytail, the woman had the kind of smooth, flawless, milk chocolate skin that said she should have been modelling skin care products instead of driving a city cab in the wee hours of the morning. Dark makeup highlighted tilted, catlike eyes, and a tiny gold ring pierced one delicate nostril. Cassie was sure she'd seen the woman before. But where?

"That'll be ten-sixty," the cabbie said, her voice lilting and exotic despite the lack of a detectable accent. Then the woman winked.

Cassie frowned.

"Wait, please," David said, distracting Cassie from her musings. "The lady's getting out, but I still need you to take me to my place."

The cabbie shrugged delicately. "If you're certain that's what you desire."

David got out of the car and offered his hand to Cassie. She took it, and forgot all about the interesting woman behind the wheel.

Finally, they stood side by side on the sidewalk. Cassie looked up at the darkened old house. Hercules lay on one of the wide stone railings that bracketed the front door. At first glance, he could almost be mistaken for a marble carving, a noble lion or maybe a fierce griffin. The lights of a passing car glinted on his damp orange fur and he looked like what he was—a large tomcat supremely annoyed to find himself outside on a drizzly night.

"Now that's a cat," David said.

"That he is," Cassie said. "Thanks for bringing me home."

He smiled crookedly. "All part of the service."

She chuckled and started up the stairs. "See you in the morning."

"See you."

He waited while she used her key to get into the entryway. Hercules streaked past her legs and ran for his kitty flap. Closing the door behind her, she saw David standing beside the cab, watching until she was safe inside. He returned her wave. She reached the first landing before she heard the cab door close and the vehicle drive away from the house.

Chapter Twelve

Kazzandra Eloeez, Princess of Par-Kerr, strode down the long hallway toward her quarters, acknowledging the greetings and bows of those she passed with a brevity that bordered on rudeness. Such an arrogant attitude was usually not her wont, but tonight, she really didn't have the patience for niceties.

The interplanetary deliberations had officially dragged past their fifth week, and the diplomatic chess game of move and countermove had reached the point of absurdity. She'd managed to be civil—barely—as she demanded a three-day recess to allow all the delegates the time to rest and clear their minds before returning to conclude the debate. She was sorry she couldn't have demanded a longer break that would have allowed her to make a quick trip home and back. She needed that more than anything.

As it stood, the majority of the delegates conceded that a three-day break was acceptable.

Par-Kerr might be a small planet in the galactic scheme of things, but no one doubted the military might of the ruling matriarchal family or the fierceness of Par-Kerr's people. Far from home, missing her comforts and her loved ones, the delegates were lucky that a raised voice was all Zandra had given them before quitting the chamber. Regretfully, she fingered the knife strapped to her leather-clad hip. The ceremonial blades worn by all daughters of the royal family had edges sharp enough to do the job, just as the exquisitely worked leather Zandra wore throat to toe served as added protection in combat. The thigh-high boots were an extravagance, true, but the tall, wide heels were comfortable and provided excellent balance.

The guards stationed outside Zandra's suite must have been warned to beware of her temper because they jumped so quickly to open the elaborate double doors that she didn't even have to slow her pace. Gifting them with a fierce smile, she swept past them, her thoughts already on a long soak in the bathing pool, followed by food and sleep. Anything to take her mind off her homesickness.

The doors slid soundlessly into place at her back, closing her inside the suite. While it was extravagant in the extreme, as far as she was concerned the suite might as well have been the meanest ten-credit-per-hour sleeping tube at the spaceport. Nothing could compare to what awaited her at home.

The pang of longing barely had time to prick her when she noticed the lights in the narrow entryway had failed to come on. Upon her arrival, she'd keyed the suite's settings herself. The lights were always supposed to activate in whatever part of the suite she occupied, unless she told the system otherwise. Zandra frowned.

"Lights," she ordered.

Nothing happened.

Silently cursing herself for her preoccupation, Zandra braced for attack. With the reflexes of a trained warrior, she unsheathed her ceremonial blade—the only weapon permitted in the council chamber—and held it at the ready. That the suite's system had malfunctioned was improbable. Far more likely that it had been programmed to ignore her commands. If it ignored her order to increase the illumination, it stood to reason it would also ignore any call for assistance. If she were inclined to make such a call. That was even more unlikely than a system malfunction. She was fully capable of defending herself.

The entryway was short, no more than a dozen paces long. It opened into the large chamber that held the bathing and relaxation area the pompous wing steward had called a grotto during her introductory tour. The grotto, in turn, led to her bedchamber. The entryway remained dark. A wavering glow at the end of the passage indicated that some sort of light source was engaged in the grotto.

Zandra heard the chiming trickle of water, followed by louder, rhythmic splashes of sound. Someone was in her bathing pool. She relaxed almost imperceptibly. It would take a bold assassin to enjoy a swim while waiting for her target to appear. Could that imbecile of a Rendari ambassador have been so bold as to ignore her rebuffs and bribe his way into her quarters? As if she would be tempted by such unexciting fare as a liaison with him, considering what she was missing in her bed.

Reminded of just that, her earlier anger and melancholy returned.

Since she wasn't a fool, she kept hold of her blade as she silently moved to the end of the entryway to survey the grotto.

There, she saw that dozens of lit candles had been spaced around the large room. Perched on shelves and in sconces, their fiery glow turned the suite's elegant, overly fussy décor into something much more primitive.

Dozens more candles floated on the surface of the heated pool. They bobbed and wobbled, never quite toppling, in the waves created by the sleek, muscled form of a swimming man. His stroking arms sliced a swift path through the tiny flames. The candles spun away, then closed over his wake to return to their positions as though guided by an unseen force—nanobots, most likely. The man moved with the sinuous grace of a powerful athlete, every few strokes turning his head aside just enough to breathe. The candlelight glimmered on the sharp planes of a clean-shaven face.

She recognized him at once. Her muscles went weak, and she almost dropped her blade.

"Davyd?"

The man in the pool came to a sudden stop. The faintly luminescent water of the shallow pool roiled around him as he stood, setting the candles dancing in the bubbling turbulence. Rivulets raced down his pleasingly haired chest and firm belly to melt into the waterline. He lifted his hands to slick black hair off his forehead and his teeth flashed in a predatory smile.

"Hello, Princess."

Before she could recover from her surprise, a muscular arm caught her around the waist and a tall, masculine body pressed against her back. A large hand took the blade from her slackened grip and her heart pounded with excitement.

"Let me put this away for you, my princess." Sharp teeth nipped her earlobe and she gasped. She'd know that deep voice anywhere, but couldn't quite believe he was here.

"Davon?"

He chuckled and loosened his grip enough to allow her to turn in his embrace. She wrapped her arms around his neck and yanked his head down, turning his chuckle into a growl of pleasure as she kissed him with all the pent-up frustration and desire caused by more than six weeks apart.

She used her tongue to push his lips open, then seduced his mouth until he couldn't resist tangling his tongue with hers. Dimly, she heard the metallic clatter as her blade hit the marble floor. Her mother, the queen, would be horrified by the sacrilege. Zandra couldn't care less as Davon's hands swept down her spine, molding her body to his naked chest and hips, lifting her ass until the needy place between her thighs cradled his swiftly hardening cock. The leather of her suit sighed as he rubbed her against his bare, warm skin.

Zandra moaned and rocked against him, barely able to control her need.

Another hard body pressed against her back, another cock nudged between her thighs. Panting, Zandra leaned away from Davon's kiss to rest her head on the shoulder of the man behind her. His hands slid to her chest to cup her breasts through the thin leather of her suit. The faint stubble on his cheeks grazed her face. His dry cheeks, she noted, without so much as a drop of water from the pool.

"And where's my kiss, sweet princess?" he asked.

She opened her eyes to focus on him. "Dev! You're here too?"

"Where else?"

With a mock sigh of regret, Davon helped her turn in his arms to face their co-consort and give him the kiss he demanded. Dev, the rogue, cupped her chin to take control of the kiss, taunting her with a warm brush of lips when she wanted to suck his tongue deep and eat him alive.

"Teasing dog," Zandra said. With a wicked smile, she pressed her hand between their bodies to take his cock in a firm grasp, squeezing the tip in precisely the way she knew made him burn. He moaned and shifted his hips away to give her better access. His eyes, laughter and hunger combined in their blue depths, stared into hers. "Now kiss me like you mean it," she breathed.

Dev's hand slid from her chin to her nape as he opened his mouth over hers. Davon ran his lips along the side of her throat. She felt the tug of his fingers on the laces that bound the corset-like top of her leather suit. She was torn between the desire to have him pick up her blade and use it to cut the damn thing from her, so she could feel their hands on her all the sooner, and the need to revel in the bliss their mere presence gave her.

Her men were here, and she was whole again.

Davyd, Davon and Dev were triplets. As was the custom on Par-Kerr, same-birth siblings were never parted, not even by mating. To bond with one was to bond with both or, in Zandra's case, all three. Though the mating had been arranged before any of them were born, Zandra had long considered herself the most fortunate of women. Not all royals were blessed enough to find love and physical paradise in the arms of their consorts. Zandra had it times three.

The crash of disturbed water reminded her that there was still one more consort who had yet to give her a proper greeting. Reluctantly, she eased away from Dev's lips. Undeterred, he simply moved his attention to her throat and the tops of her breasts.

"That's it, sweet princess," Davon said, as she leaned more firmly against his chest. He grunted in satisfaction as he tugged the last bit of lacing from the corset. The corset fell away. "There."

Dev showed his approval by tackling the sleeved garment she wore under the corset. Despite the thinness of the leather, it was as resistant to penetration as any combat armor. The snug corset had held the wraparound garment in place. Without it, the supple leather fell open. Dev spread the sides wide and freed her shoulders. The top caught on her elbows as he bent to lick the valley of flesh between her breasts.

Zandra stared over Dev's head as Davyd, water dripping down his lean body, strode to a nearby chair. The candlelight did wonderful things to the indented spheres of his buttocks, the muscles flexing as he walked. Ignoring the robe draped over the back of the chair, he picked up a large bath sheet and used it to wipe his face. He stood in profile to the three in the entryway. The water in the pool was heated, but Zandra preferred the room cool. Davyd's cock, partially hardened, seemed undaunted by any chill. She suspected that he sensed her eyes on him when he smoothed the towel down his neck with teasing sensuality.

Dev's mouth closed over her left nipple.

Zandra gasped and closed her eyes, arching helplessly toward him as he sucked strongly on the hardened tip.

Davon almost had her pants open enough to shove them down her thighs.

Her eyes shot back to Davyd. His gaze burned with obvious heat even from across the width of the pool. His cock had hardened further, but still his motions were calm and controlled as he stroked the towel down his chest. Without a word, he dropped the towel and walked to the sunken seating area.

A shaggy synth-pelt carpet covered the floor. Large pillows of varying hues of brown and gray covered a large portion of the carpet, which was a white so bright it almost hurt the eyes. Davyd ignored the pillows to go to the long couch, which was also covered in a synth-pelt. This one was smooth and short, and Zandra knew it felt velvety against bare skin. It boasted the black-and-gray stripes and swirls of a feline predator from some exotic world. Made for lounging, the couch had one armrest and half a back to lean against. A half-dozen pillar candles on tall stands bathed the area in a flickering gold wash.

Davyd seated himself squarely in the middle of the lounger, knees spread unselfconsciously wide as he draped one arm along the back.

Then, eyes never leaving hers, he wrapped the fingers of his free hand around his thickening cock and began to stroke.

Zandra bit her lip. He knew how much it excited her to watch him pleasure himself.

"Finally." Davon's voice, taut with sensual strain, rasped in her ear. He gripped the top of her loosened leather pants and pushed them over her hips. "I appreciate a well-wrapped gift as much as the next man, lover, but there's a time and a place."

As he spoke, Dev went to his knees in front of Zandra. Pressing hot, openmouthed kisses to her belly, he took over the job of easing the pants down her thighs, but was stopped by the high tops of her boots.

Zandra wiggled against Davon, trying to encourage him to let her go so they could get her out of the boots and the rest of the way out of her pants. "Let me ..."

"No," Dev said, barely lifting his mouth from her skin. "I can work with this."

Undressing almost complete, Davon brought his hands to Zandra's breasts. Holding them in slightly calloused palms—Davon was the most skilled of all of them in swordplay—he used the tips of his fingers to toy with her rigid nipples. Zandra ran her hands down the sides of his thighs and urged him closer to her. The hair on his chest rubbed enticingly against the partially bared skin of her back, some of it still covered by her dangling leather top, but the motion wasn't as enticing as the thick cock that glided in the channel between the globes of her buttocks.

On the couch, Davyd shifted to bring his other hand in play, cupping his balls as he tugged and pulled his stiff cock.

Dev's warm breath ruffled the reddish brown curls covering Zandra's pubic bone. He used his fingers to spread her nether lips until the sensation of cool air against moist flesh made her shiver. Zandra tried to widen her stance, but was limited by the stretch of leather over her lower thighs. Dev didn't seem to mind. With exquisite precision, he thrust his tongue into the exposed channel to touch her clit.

Pleasure jolted through Zandra, and she felt a flood of moisture drench Dev's fingers. He murmured in satisfaction and pressed his face harder against the restricted V of her thighs. His wicked tongue swirled around her throbbing clit, flicking it with masterful skill until her nerves practically vibrated with building pleasure.

"Oh yes," Zandra moaned. "Goddess save me. Oh, Dev, love, yes. That feels so wonderful. I need...I need... Oh..."

Davon pinched her nipples and the exquisite pain turned the last word into a low, drawn-out cry. Dev's fingers dug into her hips and he pulled her closer, his tongue never stopping the sensual torture as she came and came and came.

Chapter Thirteen

She opened her heavy eyelids to see Davyd still seated on the couch. Hands unmoving, he held the base of his cock in a tight grip, strain in his expression as he clearly fought to contain his own release.

Dev placed a gentle kiss on her belly and began to unfasten her right boot. She felt a tug on her wrist and registered that the leather blouse dangled from one arm. She let go of Davon's thigh so he could pull it the rest of the way off. He tossed it carelessly to one side. Her hair had somehow come loose from the bejeweled headdress, long, light brown curls dangling down to twine around her shoulders. Davon took care of the headdress too, pitching it away just as carelessly as he had the blouse.

Dev tugged the right boot off her leg and started on the left.

Zandra looked from one man to the other, taking in the sight of her three consorts, here, with her, where she needed them most. She didn't care if these negotiations went on for years, rather than weeks, as long as the four of them were together.

"Thank the goddess you came."

Davyd spoke for them all. "We would have come sooner, if you'd called us."

"Foolish me."

"Yes," he said gravely. "Foolish you. Come here, princess mine. I think you owe me a kiss."

Briefly, Zandra considered making him wait. Dev and Davon would be quite happy to continue their play with her and leave their brother to amuse himself. She couldn't do it. As much as she loved the playful Dev and Davon, something in the eldest triplet's more serious nature called to her. His control had a tendency to make her feel soft and feminine in a way nothing and no one else could. And when he allowed his control to slip its leash...

She gave Dev and Davon each a lingering kiss and pulled away.

Davyd's lips spread in an anticipatory smile as she stalked toward him. He released his grip on his cock and balls and again laid his arm across the couch's abbreviated back. His free hand settled on one muscled thigh, the pose one of a male predator leisurely awaiting his due. His rigid cock was anything but indifferent.

Zandra came to a stop in front of Davyd, close enough to feel his heat, scent his arousal, see the liquid glistening on the broad, flushed head of his cock. Close enough that if he wished, he could sit up and pull her into his arms. She waited to see which of them would surrender first.

After a few long heartbeats, Zandra decided she didn't want to wait.

She sank to her knees and stared into his face, a willing supplicant. Davyd's eyes gleamed under the shadow of long, dark lashes. Setting her hands on his knees, she began a slow glide up his thighs. The long muscles under the lightly-haired skin felt as hard as steel under her palms. She reached the masculine hand resting on his thigh and stopped. Her thumbs stroked circles on his inner thighs. Davyd shifted almost imperceptibly. Finally, he moved his hand to rest on the couch beside his hip. His fingers clenched into a fist, but quickly relaxed. She guessed he wanted to touch her, but held enough control to force himself not to.

She concealed a smile and resumed her exploration. As she did, her left palm skimmed over a thin weal of raised flesh. The scar, noticeably paler than his natural bronze coloring, carved a smooth path from the middle of his right thigh to hook gently around the inner curve, where it stopped just the width of a few fingers from his manhood. That scar and a small tattoo were the only noticeable differences between Davyd and his otherwise identical brothers.

She didn't always dwell on it, but sometimes the thought of how close the old injury had come to killing him brought with it a shock of fear. It hadn't, thank the Goddess. Davyd was strong, safe and healthy. And hers.

Pushing the fear away, she let her nails graze the sensitive skin of his scrotum. He sucked in an audible gasp of pleasure. Again he shifted, spreading his legs wider, sliding his ass down on the couch to ease closer to her. The lean muscles of his belly rippled, drawing her attention to the tattoo. The black dragon crouched in the hollow beside his left hip. No bigger than the tip of her thumb, the tattoo was nevertheless a work of art.

Zandra settled squarely between his spread knees. She leaned forward. Nails biting into his thighs to aid her balance, she rubbed her cheek along his cock. It shivered against her. Turning her face away, she kissed the tattoo and traced it with her tongue.

"Princess." The growled word held both warning and plea.

"Shhhhh." The second kiss, placed with diabolical care at the base of his shaft, drew a harsh sound from his throat. With the delicacy of a kitten, she licked and nibbled her way from base to tip. More liquid seeped from the slit as his passion heated.

"That's it, my little cock tease," he said. "You know exactly what I want, don't you?"

His voice broke off as she reached the thick ring of flesh just under the wide cap. She put her mouth on the exact spot that drove him wild and sucked. His hips jerked, trying to push his cock between her lips, and he cursed.

"Goddess, what you do to me."

His fingers tangled in her hair. Davyd used his grip to urge her face toward his lap. He held her firmly, but not so hard that she couldn't pull away if she wanted.

Instead, she eagerly sucked his cock into her mouth, moaning as the salty taste of him filled her senses. She played her tongue over the hot, sleek skin, swirling it around the small, seeping slit. She cupped his balls gently in one hand. Wrapping the other firmly around the base of his shaft, she began to work him with a twisting, pulling motion as she sucked.

All pretense of control gone, Davyd ran his hands from her curls down her neck, to her shoulders, then back up to cradle her face.

"Enough." His voice was almost unrecognizable. As he began to push her face away, she mumbled a protest. The muffled sound made him shudder, but he persisted until she released him and sat back on her haunches. Before she could form a more coherent protest, he picked her up with easy strength and settled her in his lap.

Zandra caught on fast. With a low laugh, she straddled his hips. She braced her hands on his shoulders as Davyd held his cock steady. She sank down, the moisture of her body making her so slick that he slid deep inside with just a single thrust. They both groaned. Davyd gripped her waist and tugged her down, harder. Zandra let him take control, guiding her up and down, up and down.

Meeting his molten stare, she looped her arms around his neck. "Now, what about my kiss, lover?"

Their mouths met hungrily, tongues tangling, teeth clicking together with the force of their passion. Zandra tried to move faster, but he held her to an even pace that drove her mad.

Then she felt something warm trickle down her spine. Instinctively, she arched toward Davyd, away from the strange sensation.

"Easy, girl." Davon. The voice, followed by the touch of familiar hands slick with oil, soothed her.

Davyd slowed her pumping hips even more until her cunt took his cock in one long, slow glide after another. Davon's palms spread the scented oil over her back, fingers working it from dewy nape to the base of her spine.

Davyd shifted, drawing Zandra onto his chest as he reclined against the couch's single arm. He bent one knee to brace his foot on the cushioned seat. The other foot remained planted on the floor. Zandra tore her mouth away from his. She couldn't resist giving his throat a passionate bite. He growled, tipping his chin back to welcome more biting kisses.

Zandra felt Davon move onto the couch behind her in the space left between Davyd's legs. He dribbled more oil onto her back. It trickled into the crack of her ass, helped along by Davon's nimble fingers. He quickly found the rosette of her anus and gently massaged it.

Zandra bucked against Davyd and gave a wordless cry of pleasure. "Steady," he said. His hands on her waist steadied her until she was almost motionless. Davon's thumb breached her anus with a shallow pumping motion. She whimpered. Davon praised her roughly and she felt his cock brush the bottom curve of her ass. He took away his thumb and she felt the stinging pleasure as he slowly pressed two fingers into her. Zandra bit her lip.

Inside her cunt, Davyd's cock seemed to grow even larger. "Zandra." He sounded like he'd said it more than once.

"Hmmm?"

"Put your elbows beside my head."

She stared at him through a haze of pleasure.

"Your elbows." Briefly, he ran his hands up her sides to where her arms clasped his neck before settling his palms back at her waist. "Brace them on the arm of the couch and lift up a bit. Perfect," he breathed as she obeyed. The position had lifted her enough that her breasts were on level with his mouth. With the barest tilt of his head, he caught one pebbled nipple with his lips and began to suck it, hard.

At the same instant, Davon removed his fingers and settled the broad tip of his cock against her anus. He kept up a steady pressure, cursing under his breath, until he breached her, quickly sliding a few inches deeper without resistance. As he pulled back, Davyd flexed his hips in a counterthrust. With the skill of experience, the brothers thrust and retreated in a rhythm that threatened to steal the thoughts from her head.

Somehow, a faint sound roused her enough from the blazing desire to force her eyes open.

Dev, patient, sweet Dev, watched them. He stood beside a pillar of colored stones, one hand braced beside a niche that held a trio of flickering candles. His chest, glistening with sweat, heaved with harsh breaths as he quickly stroked his flushed cock.

"Dev," Zandra called. "Dev, come."

Despite the intensity of his arousal, he managed to flash her a tight grin. "That's the idea."

Davyd switched his attentions to Zandra's other nipple as Davon thrust harder into her ass, faster. His sweat-dampened skin made a slapping sound as his hips smacked against her buttocks.

Zandra gave a short cry and, still supporting herself, shifted her elbows so she could sink her fingers into Davyd's hair and hold his head closer. She opened her eyes and saw that Dev hadn't moved.

"Dev, come here *now*."

In three strides, he was there, standing just behind Davyd's head. Zandra pushed up higher on her elbows and opened her mouth. He needed no further prompting to slide his cock between her lips.

The three men moved with the coordination of one mind, seeming to know intuitively when to thrust, when to pull back, when to linger and when to pound with frenzied need.

Zandra knew she couldn't hold off much longer. Pleasure shimmered through her, each thrust of her men's cocks driving her higher and higher. The grotto filled with the sound of flesh meeting flesh, with groans and cries as Zandra and her consorts strove to reach the ultimate pleasure together. Her cunt clutched at Davyd's cock greedily.

Writhing between the three men, Zandra felt the orgasm scatter her last coherent thought. Heat washed through her as rippling contractions of blissful sensation took over her cunt and belly. Her consorts came together, the three men shouting and cursing as they shook against her, their cocks jerking and pulsing as they released a rush of hot come in her ass, cunt and mouth.

Zandra swallowed Dev's come, sucking the last drop from him as he hunched over her head, fingers clenched in her hair. Davon laid his cheek against her shoulder blade, his labored breaths sending puffs of hot air along skin damp with a mix of sweat and scented oil. Beneath her, Davyd pressed a satiated kiss against her collarbone, the tender gesture drawing her attention to the sting where he'd marked her with his teeth.

Dev took an unsteady step back. She let his cock slide free of her mouth and he sank down to sit on the synth-pelt carpet. He ran a shaky hand through his dark hair, dislodging a few locks that had stuck to the sweat on his brow.

Zandra shifted her elbows from the arm of the couch and snuggled sleepily against Davyd's chest. Her face fit perfectly in the crook between his neck and shoulder. She savored the intimate scent of him and smiled.

Davon's weight left her back and his cock eased from her tingling ass.

Davyd wrapped her in his arms and bent his head to brush his lips over her cheek. The last bit of erotic tension seemed to ease from his muscles as he tightened his hold on her.

"Missed you," she said. Cradled in the safety of his embrace, she forgot all about Davon and Dev. Her lover's palm stroked over her head, smoothing the damp curls away from her face. Without thought, she added, "David."

"Sleep, sweetheart. Morning will be here soon enough."

As she felt sleep take her, she heard his low, soothing voice whisper one more word.

"Cassie."

Chapter Fourteen

Cassie stood under the hot spray and hoped the blast of water in the face would wake her up. As penance for wimping out on a cold shower, and since she didn't have an espresso maker, she also planned to stop at the coffee shop on the way to work and tell the barista to make it a double.

She couldn't explain the exhaustion weighing her down. Other than last night, all her nights this week had been early ones. Before midnight, for sure. Wasn't the need for more sleep a sign of age? And she wasn't even thirty yet, so that sucked. Except exhaustion wasn't quite the right word. She felt tired, true, but pleasantly so. Loose. Languid. That was a better word. Languid, like a purring cat stretching in a patch of sunlight.

On autopilot, she briskly washed her hair, rinsed and began to smooth the conditioner through the shoulder-length strands. Inexplicably, she found her hands slowing, fingers combing almost dreamily through her hair as her mind wandered—as it had been prone to do since she'd opened her eyes this morning—back to the snippets of fantasy that were all that remained of whatever her sleeping brain had been up to. To the best of her recollection, David had played the starring role, again. He'd also been amazingly...agile.

She paid for her inattention when a slippery ribbon of conditioner trickled into the corner of her eye. She instinctively scrunched her eyes shut, but it made the stinging worse. "Ow. Ow. Ow." She tilted her face into the flow of water and let it wash over her closed eyes. Rinsing her hands, she used her fingers to clear the last of the conditioner from her lids and lashes, then cautiously opened her eyes.

So much for loose and languid. She was definitely awake now.

Cassie quickly finished rinsing her hair, then reached for the citrus-and-ginger shower gel she favored. Squirting a generous amount into the palm of one hand, she put the tube back on the ledge of the tub and began to rub the gel into a lather. Good thing she'd set the alarm to go off early. She needed the extra time to get her head on straight.

If she didn't know better, she'd think she was coming down with something. No cough. No sniffles. No sore throat. No throbbing head. Her skin did feel kind of sensitive. Would an erotic dream cause that? Just the glide of warm water and bubbles over her bare breasts made parts of her tingle. She smoothed the lather onto her arms and shoulders. Her hands stroked over her breasts, grazing the hardened nipples. A zip of shocking pleasure raced through her and she almost slipped in the tub.

Gasping, legs unsteady, she put a hand on the white tile to help restore her balance.

Holy cow! That felt like a mini-orgasm, the kind she'd read some lucky women experienced after really great sex, when the pump, so to speak, had been well primed.

Cassie stared down at her body as if she'd never seen it before. She must really need to get laid. Maybe that would stop her sleeping self from concocting these crazy dreams starring David Michalek. Obviously, her id hadn't gotten the memo from her ego that he was off-limits. Or was that superego? At the moment, the college psych course seemed a lifetime ago. As in, when she'd last had sex. All right, so that was an exaggeration. Her body had the edge over her mind when it came to debating the wisdom of starting something with David. God, if the man could inspire half the passion in person that he did in her dreams...

Cassie reached for the knob and with a wrenching twist turned off the hot water. She shrieked as the spray instantly turned icy, but made herself stand there a full minute.

Turned out her libido *could* outlast her body. Teeth chattering, she surrendered and turned the hot water back on to finish her shower.

"Whoa, momma!" Michelle let out a wolf whistle and Cassie felt herself blush. Furtively, she scanned the waiting room and nearby glass-walled offices. It was too early for anyone to be waiting for an appointment, thank God, and no one in the offices was looking this way.

"What?" she asked, striving for nonchalance.

Michelle grinned and stood up to lean over the reception counter and give her friend an obvious head-to-toe perusal.

Cassie knew what she looked like. She'd tried on and taken off the outfit twice before deciding to wear it. It was very different from the smart-but-conservative outfits she usually wore to work. Those played down the generous breasts genetics gave her—thanks, Mom—and the slim legs she had, courtesy of hiking up and down all those stairs to her apartment.

This one didn't.

The sweetheart neckline of the soft black sweater stopped just shy of showing off her cleavage. It didn't have to, since the form-fitting cut made the most of her breasts and slender waist without coming off as trampy. She hoped. The charcoal skirt, too, was shorter and more contoured than her standard office wear. The hem brushed the tops of her knees, and a cleverly pleated split in the back drew the eye to her ass. The shoes, though, were to die for. A clever tangle of black straps and buckles, they wound around her feet to above her ankles. The style made the two-inch heels seem like three, giving the impression that she had miles of leg. Bare legs, thanks to the supersheer, superexpensive thigh-high stockings she'd defiantly smoothed on.

If people were going to talk about her (nonexistent) sex life, she'd show them sex appeal, dammit.

"Well?" Michelle asked, her eyebrow tilting expectantly.

"Can't a girl decide she wants to look pretty?"

"Not you. Little Miss Professional always has to look the corporate part. Try again."

"It's casual Friday?"

"Nuh-uh."

She knew it was a losing battle, but grimly said, "My good suit is at the dry cleaners."

Michelle laughed. "Nope."

Cassie sighed and came close enough to prop herself against the counter. Michelle settled back into her chair with a satisfied smile. She clasped her hands on her desk and beamed like a star pupil waiting to be educated.

Cassie put her heavy satchel down near her feet. She sipped her to-go cup of double espresso. Squaring her shoulders, she said, "Fine. I'm going to tell David today what my decision is."

"And? Are you going to take the job?"

"I don't know."

"You're kidding."

"I wish." Cassie toyed with the delicate gold chain that lay across her collarbones. "All I know is I have to tell him something, and I want to look my best when I do."

"Mission accomplished. You look hot. Amber Pilecky's going to want to tear your hair out."

Cassie snorted. "She already wants to tear my hair out."

"True. But now she'll want to even more."

"Then my day is complete."

They shared a grin. Cassie's felt a bit forced. She couldn't quite quell the unease that set off a kaleidoscope of butterflies in her belly. What would she tell David? She'd give it to the end of the day, then suggest they grab a coffee or something so they could talk. She'd have it figured out by then. She had to. The uncertainty was wrecking her nerves.

"Say yes," Michelle said.

"I don't know if that's the right thing to do."

"Screw the right thing. What do you know? It's a fabulous offer for a fabulous job with a guy I know you think is pretty fabulous himself." She held up a hand before Cassie could speak. "Do not say that's the problem. That's a cop-out and you know it."

"Maybe."

"No maybe about it. Say yes because you know you want to."

Shaking her head in wondering amusement, Cassie said, "How'd you get to know me so well?"

"Well, it's a combination of my keen observational skills and my ninja training. Gets the job done every time."

"Hardy-har-har."

Michelle's face sobered and she touched Cassie's hand. "Cass, I really believe you're overthinking things here. Take the job. If it works out, great. If it doesn't," she shrugged, "quit and find something else. But if you don't do this, I know you're going to regret it."

"You're probably right." At Michelle's skeptical stare, she said, "Okay, you're definitely right. I'd regret it. Probably."

Feeling like she was taking the coward's way out, Cassie bent to pick up her satchel. "I'm still going to take the rest of the day to think things over. I'd better head to my desk. I've got a ton of stuff to finish up before the sword of Damocles falls."

"Fine. Lunch?"

"I'll have to let you know. Depends on how much my to-do list has grown overnight."

"Give me a buzz, either way."

Nodding, Cassie turned to go. She noticed for the first time that Michelle's thick hair was pulled back in a tight ponytail. And it was damp. Her friend was obsessive about blow-drying and styling her hair every morning. She said if she didn't, the curls went wild and were impossible to control. And Cassie knew Michelle almost never wore her hair up because she said it gave her a headache. So why was she this morning?

"Why is your hair wet?"

Michelle stilled. "What?"

"I just wondered, why is your hair wet?"

Cassie watched the blush creep from Michelle's cheeks and down her neck. Even the tips of her ears reddened. Interesting.

"There's not a cloud in the sky," Cassie said, drawing the words out. "Sidewalks aren't even damp, so I couldn't have missed a cloudburst. Hmmm."

"I, uh."

"Zak and Steve get you home okay last night?"

"Uh—"

The phone rang. Michelle pounced on it. "Good morning, Stockton Enterprises. How may I help you?"

She touched the headset and sent Cassie what was apparently meant to pass for a distracted wave. Cassie savored her espresso, not to mention the role reversal, and made no move to leave.

Michelle transferred the caller and disconnected. Mutely, she watched Cassie with the eyes of a startled deer. "Well," she finally said in an overbright tone. "You said you've got a lot of things to do today. And I've got," she gestured at her regimentally organized desk, "things, you know, to do."

Cassie refused to budge. She quirked her eyebrow. "Well?"

"What?"

"Let's see." Cassie tapped her lips with her index finger, as though considering. "Michelle says, 'Can't a girl decide she wants to look pretty.' No, that one doesn't fit. Michelle says, 'It's casual Friday.' Better, but not quite it, I'm thinking."

Before she could say anything else, Michelle leapt to her feet and plastered her hand over Cassie's mouth. "All right, all right, Miss Nosy Pants. I'll tell you all about it, but not here. Later."

Cassie tugged her friend's wrist enough to free her mouth for a muffled, "When and where?"

Defeated, Michelle let her hand drop. "Lunch. If you're free. We'll go for a walk. Away from here."

"As of now, I can *definitely* do lunch."

"Wonderful."

"Oooh. I can't wait to hear all the details! Which one was it? Zak?"

Michelle bit her lip.

"Steve?"

Michelle looked down at her clasped hands, but Cassie saw her lips twitch into the ghost of a smile.

"*Both* of them?" Expecting her friend to deny it, she could only stare, wide-eyed and slack-jawed, when Michelle didn't. Cassie crowed, "Michelle, you bad, bad girl!"

Michelle shushed her and whispered, "Cassie, drop it! Later, I promise."

The uncertainty over her looming decision about David's job offer temporarily forgotten, Cassie nodded emphatically. "Oh, you better, girlfriend. I can't wait."

Still smiling, Cassie walked down the hall toward her cubicle. She hoped the suit she'd dropped off at the cleaners before work really would be ready at the end of the day. She'd wear it Monday morning for their trip to Chicago. That reminded her: if there wasn't a confirmation waiting in her e-mail in-box when she logged in, she'd have to check on their flight reservations. And run the file up to Legal so the changes David needed could be made. Then coordinate meetings and a temporary workspace for while they were in Chicago.

Mind busy with plans for the coming trip, Cassie began to rummage in her satchel with one hand for her planner. Her head was still down when she stepped into her cubicle. She smelled the perfume an instant before it registered that she wasn't alone. She came to a full stop and stared.

Amber Pilecky jerked upright so quickly, the chair she sat in—Cassie's chair—rolled a foot away from the desk. Cassie's eyes went to the key still stuck in the lock of her bottom drawer, the one Amber had been hunched over. Without a word, Cassie pulled her own keys from the reserved pocket in her satchel. Dangling the jangling ring, she noted her desk key in its usual place. Her eyes narrowed on Amber.

"Cassie. You're early." Acting for all the world as though she hadn't just been trying to break into Cassie's desk with a duplicate key, Amber stood up and straightened her too-short skirt.

Cassie felt a brief moment of satisfaction as the other woman took in Cassie's sexy outfit. Amber's brightly painted lips thinned. The satisfaction disappeared in a flash as Cassie's mind began clicking over things. She'd been right. Amber *had* been in her cubicle last night. She hadn't even had to lower herself to jimmying the desk lock, not if she had a duplicate key. It confirmed Cassie's suspicion that Amber had deliberately hidden the package from the Legal Department.

Amber started to stalk out of the cubicle. Cassie sidestepped to block her. Amber stared haughtily down her surgeon-enhanced nose. Cassie held out her hand.

"Key," she demanded.

"I beg your pardon?"

"That's right, you should beg my damn pardon. Later. For now, I'll settle for the key I just saw you grab."

Amber huffed and tried to leave the cubicle again.

Without thinking twice about it, Cassie dropped her coat and satchel and grabbed Amber's arm. Amber let out a startled cry. Cassie held up the mostly empty to-go cup of lukewarm espresso and tilted it threateningly toward Amber's expensive-looking blouse. Dropping her voice into a threatening growl, she said, "Listen, you witch. Give me the damn key or I dump this very dark, very hot coffee all over you. And that's just for starters."

"You wouldn't."

"Today, I would. It's been a very strange week, and you're at the top of my lump-of-coal list. Try me."

It was a standoff. Amber tried to maintain her cool, but Cassie's unwavering glare seemed to unnerve her. Grudgingly, Amber held up her fist, but made no move to release the key. Cassie tilted the cup a fraction more in mute threat.

"Fine," Amber spat. She opened her clenched fingers to reveal the shiny silver key. Cassie let her go and snatched the key from her palm.

Amber shoved past her. "You are such a nutcase. You just wait. I'm going to complain about this. You threatened me. Assaulted me. You'll be getting a call."

"You do what you have to do, and I'll do what I have to do."

"What's that supposed to mean?"

Cassie let out a disgusted sigh. She snatched up her coat and satchel and flung them onto her chair. "Just get out of here, Amber. I really can't deal with you right now. I've got too much to do today." As if in confirmation, the phone rang. Cassie glanced at the call display, and knew she had to answer it. With one last fulminating glare at Amber, she answered with a deliberately upbeat, professional tone. "Rebecca. You must have read my mind. I was just going to give you a call."

Without waiting to see if Amber would leave, Cassie sat down, scooted her chair up to her desk, and picked up a pen and notepad. "I got your e-mail yesterday, and I just wanted to double-check some of the figures with you. They're on page thirty-seven. You've got it in front of you? Fantastic."

The carpeted floor wasn't up to the stomp of stilettos as Amber made her escape.

Chapter Fifteen

If someone had had a video camera running, Cassie could chalk her day up to an epic fail and get rich off the Internet ads once it went viral.

First, Legal gave her a hassle about the changes David had ordered for the paperwork for Chicago. She'd had to patiently explain that, no, they couldn't wait until Monday. It wasn't her fault that the legal eagle in charge of the section in question had decided to take an unscheduled golf day. He'd just have to come in from the links to get the work done like a regular person.

Then, there was a mix-up with their reservations. As in, the Travel Department hadn't made them. Cassie ran down to the second floor to personally hand over a copy of the e-mail she'd sent from home before going to bed. Tina assured her that she'd have the flight information by the time she got back to her desk and that a car would be waiting to pick Cassie and David up at O'Hare bright and early Monday morning.

Running into Lou Miller in the photocopier room was a special treat. Like Michelle, he approved of Cassie's outfit. Unlike her friend, his leer was real. And a little creepy. He refused to accept her more subtle refusals to join him for a drink after work tonight, tomorrow night, next week, sometime soon, or any time of the day or night she cared to pick up the phone.

The man had no concept of personal space. She had to actively control a shudder when he touched her elbow in what he apparently considered a flirty move. She'd been forced to be blunt and tell him it would never happen, and to just leave her alone. He'd contrived to look hurt and insulted, apologized for bothering her with his "friendly" invitation, and stalked out. Which made her angrier—what gave him the nerve to try to make her feel guilty for turning him down? A woman had a right to go about her business without being harassed. So what if his marriage was over—okay, she was, admittedly, a romantic who totally believed in hearts and flowers and happily ever after. She did still feel a little sorry about it. But did that give him a free pass to be an obnoxious pig?

She couldn't even get five minutes' peace to treat herself to a chocolate bar from the vending machine. She walked into the half-filled breakroom, noted a sudden hush. No one would meet her eye. To make matters worse, Amber and Diane Somerfield from HR, seated together at one small table, looked pretty cozy with their heads together.

Cassie didn't know how she could have forgotten about the gossip Amber had been spreading. Of course people were still talking about Cassie and David. As she well knew, the more salacious the rumor, the harder it was to shake. Never mind that she and David were consenting adults and whatever they chose to do together was no one else's business. People would still talk. Today's sexy wardrobe choice suddenly seemed like not such a great idea. She turned right around and walked out of the breakroom.

David had been buried under his own mountain of work all morning, and they'd barely had time to exchange more than two words each time she hurried into his office to drop something off or pick something up. She also hadn't quite found the nerve to ask if he'd be able to grab a coffee with her at the end of the day so she could respond to his job offer. She decided she'd send him an e-mail about it. Later.

Cassie wound up spending so much time on the phone putting out sparks before they could turn into fires that she had to skip lunch with Michelle. That put the cherry on the crap sundae of her day. She had really wanted to hear about what she'd privately termed Michelle and Zak and Steve's Excellent Adventure. Thankfully, she was too busy to let her imagination run away with her on that. She'd have to pump Michelle for all the details after her meeting with David.

Which she still hadn't e-mailed him to schedule.

By two, she was reaching for the bottle of painkillers in her top drawer. Her head and neck throbbed with a tension headache that wouldn't let up. The trilling electronic jangle of the phone made her fumble the bottle. She grabbed for it, but only managed to tip it on the way down. She stared at the white pills scattered over the worn carpet under her desk like hailstones. "Perfect. Just perfect."

She slumped back in her chair, pressed the heel of her hand into her forehead and closed her eyes. The phone warbled again. She wanted nothing more than to let the call go to voice mail. But what if it was important? Without checking the caller ID, she snatched the phone out of the cradle.

Briskly, she said, "This is Cassie Parker."

"Cassie Parker. You *bitch.*"

Startled by the venom in the unfamiliar voice, Cassie could only say, "Excuse me?"

"Excuse you? Never! You listen to me, you bitch..."

Trying to interrupt the woman's tirade was like trying to stop a telemarketer midspiel. As the woman continued to rant, Cassie began to get a glimmer of an idea of who her caller was. "Mrs. Roland?"

The woman let out a strangled gasp of outrage. "So you're fucking so many married men you can't keep track of them? Amber told me all about you, Miss Parker."

The light dawned. Amber, Roland's office candy and current bed buddy, had tossed Cassie to the man's wife as *the other woman.*

"Now hold on, Mrs. Roland—"

"No, you hold on! You will regret trying to steal my husband. If you think he'll leave me for you, you are as much deluded as you are a slut."

Cassie listened numbly as the dial tone in her ear turned into an annoying beep. Slowly she set the receiver back on the cradle and leaned back. The pills on the floor crunched under the wheels of her chair and she winced.

What should she do? The CEO's wife thought Cassie was sleeping with her husband. Not a good enemy to have. And it was all Amber's fault, the lying bitch.

Emotions swirled inside her, too many to pin one down. She felt off balance, as though she were watching this sadistic farce happen to someone else. The phone rang, further rattling her frazzled nerves. Warily, she eyed it. Thankfully, the four-digit number on the display indicated it was from an internal caller. Unfortunately, the screen didn't identify the caller by name.

Resigned, she picked it up. "Hello?"

"Hey, Cassie." The voice on the other end was breezy and feminine. "It's Diane."

"Diane?"

"Diane Somerfield. In HR?"

Amber's friend, Cassie thought. Her roiling emotions swirled faster. "Oh, right."

"Can you stop by my office for a few minutes?"

"Your office?"

"Uhm-hmm. It'll be really quick, I promise. There's just something I need to talk to you about." The woman spoke more quickly. "It's kind of important, nothing to worry about, but if you could come by and see me, that would be great."

"Now's not a good time, Diane. I'm kind of in the middle of some—"

"I won't take up much of your time, I promise. See you soon. Bye!" Diane sang the last word as though it had two syllables.

Frowning, Cassie put the phone back on its cradle. Her hand shook. She felt sick to her stomach. Too many things were going on that were out of her control, and she didn't know how to handle it.

Maybe Amber had complained to HR about that scene with the key. Well, fine. Let her. It wasn't like she could justify rummaging through Cassie's desk in the first place. Besides, Cassie hadn't really hurt the whiny drama queen. And it wasn't like there was much espresso left in the cup she threatened to pour on the other woman. Cripes, it hadn't even been hot.

Cassie shook her head, trying to organize her thoughts. Why the hell was she worried about getting reprimanded for threatening Amber with an almost-empty cup of lukewarm espresso when the bitch had sicced Mrs. Roland on her with a truly nasty lie?

Rage began to coalesce in the maelstrom of Cassie's confused emotions.

She stood up and marched out of her cubicle. The HR offices were down a different hall, branching away from Reception. Michelle looked up as she walked by.

"What's up?"

"Amber's pal in HR wants to see me."

Michelle frowned. "That can't be good."

Tight-lipped, Cassie shook her head.

Six clerks worked in the HR Department's outer office. Three higher-level workers occupied glass-walled offices along one side of the room, while the manager of human resources rated a fully enclosed, private office at the back. The clerk in the desk closest to the door looked up.

She pointed to the first office, where they could both see Amber's friend tapping away on her keyboard, staring intently at her monitor. "Diane's waiting for you."

"Thanks." Cassie walked into the office without knocking.

Diane turned from the monitor and smiled. "Cassie, hi. Close the door, please."

Cassie did, then took the proffered guest chair. It took some effort to prevent herself from bolting up out of it. "If this is about this morning," she started, "that wasn't entirely my fault. And I've got a doozy of a complaint of my own."

"This morning?"

Maybe Amber hadn't made a complaint. "Never mind. You go first. What was it you wanted to see me about?"

Diane folded her hands on her desk and assumed a serious expression. She didn't speak for a long moment, then sighed. "This is really kind of awkward, so I'll just get right to the point."

"I'd appreciate that."

"It concerns your...well, your conduct, I guess you could say."

"My conduct?"

"Yes. With our consultant, David Michalek."

Cassie could only stare.

Diane continued, "We've received some complaints that your behavior in the office hasn't been very," she paused, apparently searching for the right word, "professional.

"You see, Cassie, what employees do on their own time is their own business. While the company would prefer that employees didn't become involved with each other outside of working hours, it's not something we actively restrict here at Stockton."

Mortification joined the growing fury washing through Cassie, making her glad for the chair holding her up. This couldn't be happening. She was being censured—by God, officially reprimanded, it seemed—for something else that hadn't even happened.

As Diane nattered on, Cassie found herself focusing on the other woman's flashy wedding set. She was a hand-talker. Now that the ice had been broken, she used her hands to gesture as she made each point about propriety and code of conduct and consideration for one's coworkers. She had strong hands, with wide palms and well-tended nails. The multidiamond ring set with wide gold bands made her fingers look stubby.

Cassie knew she should probably say something, defend herself, but she couldn't think how to begin. She spared a brief thought for the closed door. At least no one else could hear her being dressed down. Was she going to be fired? Surely a senior manager would have to be involved if that was the case, rather than just a talk with an HR associate.

Her mind flashed to a mental snapshot of Diane and Amber, thick as thieves, huddled together in the breakroom just a few hours ago. Amber, who never missed a snide swipe or jab. Amber, who Michelle said was spreading nasty rumors about her and David. Amber, who she'd caught just that damn morning trying to break into her desk, and she had no doubt it wasn't the first time, either. Amber, who told Mrs. Roland that Cassie was sleeping with the CEO.

Her emotions crystallized into outraged fury.

That witch. *She set me up.*

She interrupted Diane midsentence.

"Can't restrict."

Thrown off her stride, Diane frowned in confusion. "I beg your pardon?"

"You mean you *can't* place restrictions on what people do away from the office. It's not in the employee handbook, and even if it were, it's not the kind of thing you could actually enforce without things turning ugly. There's that pesky little matter of rights. Privacy. That kind of thing."

"That's neither here nor there, since what I'm talking about definitely *is* the company's business, since it *is* happening on company time."

Cassie's fingers dug into the arms of her chair as she forced herself to stay seated. This, on top of everything else she'd had to deal with today? No, forget today. This whole week had been a whole lot of crazy, tied up with a bow, waiting to explode in her face. "What are you talking about?"

"You were seen, more than once, Cassie. Really, you can't expect the company to turn a blind eye to that kind of thing. Most places would consider it a firing offense. I'm doing you a favor by starting with a warning."

"Seen doing what? Exactly."

Diane blushed and her eyes darted away. "Well, it has to do with you and Mr. Michalek, and..."

"And?"

The other woman bit her lip, obviously embarrassed. Cassie insisted, "Diane, if I'm going to be accused of something, I want to know what it is. In detail. Just so there are no misunderstandings."

"Fine. You were seen having sex with Mr. Michalek in his office. And the ladies' washroom on the third floor. And in the copy room. Someone working late saw you on that occasion."

Cassie had moved way past fury. Softly, she said, "Seen. By whom?"

The woman refused to speak.

"So I'm to be accused of unprofessional, stupid, disgusting behavior—I mean, sex in the office?—and I don't even get to know who's slandering me?"

Before she realized what she was doing, Cassie had leapt to her feet. Bracing her palms on Diane's pristine desk, she leaned toward the other woman. Diane sat up so abruptly, her chair squeaked in protest.

"You are actually giving me a warning about something that I haven't even done, based on the word of that skanky slut Amber Pilecky? Are you serious?"

"Cassie, please. There's no need to raise your voice, and I certainly don't appreciate—"

"Raise my voice? You dare to sit there, accusing me of sleeping with David Michalek at work, and you expect me to just take it? I have never stinted on one iota of work for this company. I've rarely called in sick. I've worked hundreds of hours of overtime, without pay, without complaint. I've gone above and beyond my job description, because you know what, Diane? I take pride in my work. I am a *professional*."

Diane inched her chair away from her desk. Cassie, ignoring the cornered-rabbit look in the other woman's eyes, straightened and put her hands on her hips.

"Speaking of *professional*, how's this, Diane? Maybe if you did your damn job instead of acting like Amber Pilecky's trained attack poodle, you'd pay more attention to some of the situations that really do stink up your yard. Like maybe, oh..." Cassie tapped her finger on her chin and pretended to think. "Let's start with Lou Miller, shall we? Just today, I practically had to tase the guy to get him to catch a clue to the fact that I will never, ever, if-the-sun-were-going-to-explode-tomorrow *ever* date him. And I'm not the only woman he's harassing on a daily basis. The man's a slimy pig who can't get it through his skull that when a woman says no, she means no, and don't keep asking until she changes her mind or loses it. If you were doing your job, Diane, he'd be the one in here getting a 'warning,' not me. I will so laugh my ass off when you're staring down the barrel of a multi-complainant sexual harassment suit."

"Well, I—"

Cassie couldn't seem to stop. Manic energy coursed through her body. Her skin tingled, her heart pounded and she had to keep moving. Diane's office was small, but there was enough room, barely, to pace four steps one way, spin on her heel, and pace four steps back. She pointed a finger at Diane, who flinched as though she'd pulled a gun. "And let's not forget Mo Zimalli in Advertising. Wonder why he isn't meeting his sales targets? Well, no one else is, since it's pretty much an accepted fact that he's managing his family's restaurant franchise on company time, using the fax machine to send product orders, talking on the phone to suppliers, setting the day's specials. God, he even used the small conference room to interview for servers. Ever investigate that, Diane?"

"Actually—"

"And how about those gift cards that came in after we landed the massive deal with the national coffee chain. You know, the cards that were supposed to be given to the staff who worked on the deal, but actually went to the manager's fantasy league buddies." Cassie snorted. "Yeah, you didn't think we knew about that, huh? Big mistake. This place is like a nosy little town. Everyone knows everyone else's business."

Cassie paused for breath. Diane used the opportunity to get up from her chair and edge toward the door.

"You've brought up some really good points, Cassie. Why don't we make an appointment to talk about this next week?"

Smoothly, Cassie stepped to the side, blocking the door. Diane, who was a good six inches taller than Cassie and looked like she spent a fair amount of time in the gym, wilted back to her position behind the desk.

"I'm not quite done yet," Cassie said. "I think you wanted to talk about my professional conduct, right? So let's talk about my conduct.

"Want to know who I just fielded a call from? Genevieve Roland. Yeah, that's right. I'm sure I looked pretty horrified too. Hard to say for sure, since I was too busy trying to figure out why the hell she was laying into me. I've never even met the woman. In between the curses and tears, she managed to tell me that Amber said I was chasing after her husband. That's funny, don't you think? I mean, considering that the security tape posted on YouTube clearly shows who was really putting the froth on his morning latte in the elevator. Being a professional, I didn't share that little tidbit with poor Mrs. Roland. Frankly, I didn't know how to handle it. I think I'll leave that little treat to you.

"You *dared* to call me in here to talk about my professional conduct? Now there," Cassie wagged her finger, "there I think we might have a bit of a conflict of interest. Because everything else aside, the thing I think the execs might find the most immediately alarming is the fact that Amber somehow had a key that gave her access to sensitive documents locked in my desk. Since HR is the one department that has duplicate keys for employees' desks, I wonder what anyone looking for the second key might find? Don't you think they'd be just a little pissed that someone in HR might have helped Amber Pilecky fuck with a project that's worth hundreds of millions of dollars to the company? And do you know *who* they might be looking at in HR?"

Diane quailed. Cassie smiled. "Exactly."

Behind her, the door was shoved forcefully open. Cassie was so fired up, she didn't even bother to see who had come in the office. The sound of his voice snapped her attention to him.

"Cassie," David said. His hand wrapped around her left biceps. "I've been looking for you everywhere. We've got that meeting to get to."

"Meeting? I don't—"

"Yes. Right now, or we're going to be late." He gave Diane a charming smile. "Sorry I have to take her away while you're chatting, but we've got business to attend to. You don't mind, do you?"

Diane couldn't talk fast enough. "No, of course not. We're done here. Take Cassie with you. Please."

Before Cassie could protest, David had turned her around. Hand manacling her arm, he marched her through the office and into the hall. As they went, Cassie noticed that not only did they have the rapt attention of the HR clerks at their desks, but also that of easily another dozen people trying to give the impression that they had a reason to be there.

She refused to make eye contact. She was still angry at Diane, furious with Amber—but some of that anger turned to chagrin. Just how loud had she gotten during her rant?

"David, I'm so sorry. I must have forgotten about the meeting. What was it for?"

"There's no meeting." His voice sounded choked. Oh God. He must be furious that he had to take her in hand like an unruly child bullying the little kids at the schoolyard.

"Oh. Well. That's good, then. Look, I guess I'd better start cleaning out my desk–"

She lifted her arm, to remind him he still held it. David ignored the hint and kept walking. He was moving so quickly, she practically had to skip to keep up. Since he kept his gaze straight ahead, his face was in profile. He didn't appear to be angry. His neck and ears were a little flushed though.

"Why?" he asked.

"Isn't it obvious? I'm going to get fired. After that little show, I'm sure they won't want me around."

David made an odd sound in his throat.

"Are you all right?"

He didn't say anything, just pulled her into the reception area. Cassie was surprised to see Michelle waiting for them. "Here you go," she said, handing David the coat and satchel Cassie had left in her cubicle.

"Thanks, Michelle," he said.

Cassie didn't get a chance to say anything. David towed her through Reception and straight to the elevator. As if on cue, the doors slid open and they stepped inside the empty car.

Cassie started to feel queasy again, thanks to the sick swirl of emotions twisting inside her. Anger was still there, all right. So was embarrassment, mortification, outrage and a good dose of helplessness.

The doors slid silently closed. As soon as they did, David let go of her arm and put his hand to his face.

Though he'd done a good impression of a knight in shining armor, saving her from disaster, Cassie realized he must be feeling overwhelmed too. It couldn't have been pleasant having to drag the raving lunatic he'd been working with out of the office. He must be thanking his lucky stars she hadn't accepted his job offer yet. Now he'd have a chance to rescind it.

Add sad to the emotional soup.

Cassie hung her head. "I'm so sorry you had to see that."

His shoulders shook. He made that odd choking sound again. Then, as if he couldn't hold it back any longer, he burst out laughing. His hand dropped from his face, and she realized his eyes twinkled with mirth. "I'm just sorry I missed the start of it. 'Putting the froth on his morning latte'?" He lost it again, laughing almost helplessly.

"You heard that, huh?"

He nodded. Amusement threaded his tone as he said, "Cass, the entire fifth floor heard it. You'd kind of progressed beyond the dulcet-tones stage. Why do you think they were all so goggle-eyed?"

"Well. That's embarrassing."

That set him off again.

Watching him, Cassie smiled. Her smile spread and she began to laugh. "It was kind of satisfying. Getting all that off my chest. If you gotta go, go with a bang."

He put an arm around her shoulders and gave her a friendly hug. "Cassie Parker, I have the feeling you do everything with a bang." A soft bell tone followed by a gentle bump announced their arrival on the ground floor. The elevator doors slid open. Keeping his arm around her, David ushered her into the lobby. "Let's get you home."

Chapter Sixteen

The ring of keys crashed to the floor with a metallic jangle. Flustered, Cassie bent to scoop them off the scuffed wooden floorboards beside her welcome mat.

"You know, you really don't have to do this," she said to David as she jammed the appropriate key in the lock with more than necessary force. "I know you've probably got a million things to do."

He dipped his head to take a long sniff of the large brown-paper sacks he held in his arms. "And miss out on the Golden Dragon's dumplings and General Tao's chicken? I'm starving. Besides, you don't want to have to eat all this yourself, do you?"

"It would take me a week to eat all that by myself. What possessed you to buy so much?"

He shrugged. "I'm hungry. This'll be the first real meal I've had since breakfast."

Cassie opened her door and he followed her in, shoving it closed with his heel. In defiance of her resolution to pick up after herself, Cassie dumped her satchel beside the closet door and piled her coat on top of it.

"Here, let me take those so you can get out of your coat." Cassie took the paper sacks from him and headed for the kitchen. Sighing, she set the bags on the counter. Instead of unpacking them, she opened the fridge and took the bottle of wine from the shelf in the door. The fancy label made her pause. It was the Chilean wine she'd opened Monday night. The one she suspected might be off, since she'd had a truly bizarre dream after drinking a few glasses of the stuff. The details were hazy, but she did remember the dream had been really weird.

There was more wine left than she'd expected. More than half a bottle. Holding the door of the fridge open with her hip, she pried the cork out and took a cautious sniff.

"Wine? Great idea."

The sound of David's voice right behind her made Cassie jump a little. Turning, she saw he'd taken off his trench coat and his suit jacket. He'd also loosened his tie enough to unfasten the top button of his shirt. She'd always thought of him as tall and lean, but he seemed to take up a lot of space in her galley kitchen. Her eyes fastened on the strong, tanned column of his throat. His jaw looked a little rough as the stubble of late afternoon defeated his morning shave, especially in the tiny hollow of the cleft in his chin. She wanted to nibble it.

"Are you all right?"

Stop lusting after him, Cassie! "Fine. Just jumpy, I guess. It was a crazy day, to say the least." She stepped back enough to let the door close. The loss of the fridge's glow made the small kitchen seem even more intimate. She walked to the sink and flipped on the light mounted under the cabinet, instead of the bright overhead. "We'll have to do without wine, I'm afraid. I think this stuff might have gone bad."

"Really?" David took the open bottle and held it to his nose. "Smells good to me. I'm willing to risk it if you are."

Cassie shrugged off her misgivings. She was being silly, all because of one bad dream...followed by three really spectacular ones. "Why not?" she said, opening the cupboard above the sink and taking down a couple of large-bowled wineglasses. *"Live Dangerously.* Maybe that should be my new motto."

"I could get on board with that." David unbuttoned the cuffs of his pale blue dress shirt and began rolling up the sleeves, exposing the ropy muscles of his forearms. "I'll put the food out while you set the table."

"Sure thing." Cassie gathered plates and cutlery. She reached for the paper towels, then shrugged. *Live dangerously,* she reminded herself, and opened a drawer to take out her fancy woven place mats and a couple of linen napkins.

She began arranging the settings on the table. David asked, "Mind if I put some music on?"

She directed him to the digital music player in the living room and returned to the kitchen for candles and a set of fancy holders she'd never taken out of the box. Since she was a sucker about buying the damn things at candle parties, she might as well get some use out of them.

Finally, they were both seated at the café table she barely used. The place mats, candleholders and assortment of cardboard cartons and foil takeout containers covered the tabletop. Other than the low light she'd left on in the kitchen, and the glow of the streetlights that barely touched her windows, the candles were the sole illumination in the apartment. Cassie shifted in her seat and her knee brushed David's under the table.

"Sorry. This was the only kind of table I could really fit in here. I know the apartment's small, but I fell in love with it." She shrugged.

He smiled. "No problem. I think I'll live. You ready to eat?" He picked up one of the cartons and opened it. "And these would be your chicken balls."

Reacting to his teasing tone, she snatched the carton away from him. "I happen to like chicken balls."

"So does my seven-year-old nephew." He handed her a Styrofoam cup. "Don't forget your syrup."

"That's cherry sweet-and-sour sauce, thank you very much. Besides, you're one to talk, with your lemon chicken. That comes with sweet sauce."

"Lemon, as in, made with real lemons. If your cherry sauce came into any contact with a real live cherry, it was probably by purest accident."

"Ha-ha." Cassie rolled a few chicken balls onto her plate and made a production out of drizzling cherry sauce over them. It was strange, but she was almost able to forget about the horrible scene at work. She knew she had David to thank for that.

He held up a pair of chopsticks. "Live dangerously?" he invited.

Laughing, she shook her head. "Uh, no. I'm too hungry to chase my food around my plate, hoping to spear it."

He set the chopsticks aside and began to open the rest of the cartons and foil containers. As they filled their plates, he said, "Before you decided on *Live Dangerously*, what was your previous motto?"

"Hmmm? Oh, motto. Right." She concentrated on cutting a chicken ball without sending it shooting off her plate like a greased Ping-Pong ball. "I guess it was something like *Don't Rock the Boat*. Or maybe *Good Things Come to Those Who Wait*. How 'bout you?"

He popped a spiced shrimp into his mouth and chewed thoughtfully. "*Make Your Own Opportunities*."

"That's a good one."

He shrugged. "It's true enough. The way I see it, it's the only way to get what you want out of life. If I'm not willing to go for what I want, why should the universe make things happen for me?"

"And it works for you?"

He toasted her with his wineglass. "So far."

It wasn't until they'd finished that David brought up what she'd mentally decided to call The Incident.

Throughout dinner he'd managed to keep her laughing and her mind off The Incident. Aside from their serendipitous meeting at the bar last night, it was the first opportunity she'd had to spend any length of time with him without a work schedule cutting things short. He showed none of the little signs that indicated he had somewhere to be. No surreptitious peeks at his watch, no shifting in his chair or uncomfortable glances at the door.

"So, what are you going to do?"

"About?"

His expression told her he knew she was being deliberately obtuse. She sighed. Picking up the wine bottle, she tilted it to see how much was left. Not as much as she wished for this discussion. Still, she carefully divided it between their glasses. There was just enough to fill each glass about a quarter of the way to the rim.

"Honestly? I have no idea. Besides, they're probably going to fire me, at which point, it's out of my hands."

"If you want to stay, I'm sure you can. You made some valid points there. They'd have a lot of explaining to do if they fired you for doing nothing more than telling the truth."

Cassie sighed. "I don't know. It might have felt good getting all that crap off my chest, but it also made me realize that there are a lot of things I just can't stand about that place anymore. They've got a really skewed way of handling some things. A lot of favoritism."

He nodded. "There is that."

"You see that a lot? I mean, as a consultant. You know, all the dirty laundry stuff. Affairs, backstabbing, gossiping, just general nastiness."

"Of course. People are people, after all. Things get messy. But that's one of the best things about being a consultant."

"How's that?"

"I get to go in, tell companies how they should be doing things, shake things up a bit. But I'm still my own boss. If it's a crap company, I have the option of never doing business with them again. Once the contract's done, I'm outta there."

"Pay's good too, huh?"

He grinned. "Good enough."

"Hmmm."

"Another thing to remember is that there are way more worthwhile people out there than there are cheats, backstabbers and nasty gossips."

"I guess that's true." She wrinkled her nose. "Logically, I know it is. It's just hard to get past things like what happened today."

"You said something about Rolly's wife laying into you?"

"God, don't remind me. I don't even want to think about what she said."

"That bad, huh? I wouldn't worry about it too much, though."

Cassie pushed a grain of rice around her plate with her fork. "Why?"

"I happen to know Amber isn't going to skate on this one. Someone sent the URL of the video you mentioned to the board of trustees. Rolly will have some explaining to do."

172

She lost interest in the rice. Surprise made her blurt, "For getting a blow job in the elevator?"

"There might have been some unsanctioned use of company expense accounts—trips, expensive gifts, that kind of thing. They're trying to keep it quiet."

"I don't believe it. Well, sort of. I mean, I knew Amber was involved with Roland, but I had no idea it was so...soap opera. And it's all blowing up because someone sent a video URL to the board." She shook her head.

"Several someones," David said. "Rolly and Amber weren't as discreet as they liked to think. The elevator thing was just the icing on the cake. You can bet Amber won't be at Stockton much longer. With the trouble facing Rolly, she'll need another bank account to latch on to."

"Who sent the video?"

"I'll never tell."

"You have to."

"It's possible I could be convinced."

Cassie dropped her chin and reminded herself, again, that he was just being a nice guy, *not* coming on to her. It sure seemed like he was coming on to her, though. She rubbed her hand over her forehead. Holding her bangs out of the way, she huffed out a sigh. *Get a grip. At least Amber will be out of a job too.*

"Have you given any thought to my offer?"

Her head jerked up and she stared into his eyes. "What?"

"Cassie, I still want you to come work for me."

"Even after today?"

"Why wouldn't I?"

"You don't think I'm nuts? That I'd go on some crazy tirade and chase off your clients?"

He laughed. "Do you make a habit of it?"

"Well, no. That was kind of my first time."

"No, Cass, I don't think you'd chase off my clients. The way I see it, everyone's entitled to one blowout. Like I said before, more than once, you're an intelligent, talented woman. Any company would be lucky to have you. That's why I want you for mine."

"David, I don't know. This has been a really strange day. Strange week," she muttered.

"What was that?"

She waved her hand as if erasing her last words from an invisible chalkboard. "Nothing. Never mind. I really want to say yes, David—"

"Great! It's settled then."

Exasperated, she said, "David. I really want to say yes, *but* I think I should take some more time to consider things. I don't want to do something either of us will regret."

He frowned, but seemed to realize he wouldn't get anywhere if he pushed. "Fine. But I'm not going to regret it if you come work for me, Cassie."

"David..."

He held up his hands in mock surrender. "All right, all right. I won't mention it again. Tonight."

Cassie shook her head. His persistence amused her, but it wouldn't do any good to let him see her weakness. He'd press his advantage if he sensed she'd cave and accept his offer with just a smidgen more effort on his part. He was nothing if not charming and tenacious. Those traits were part of what made him such an effective consultant.

"I'd better start wrapping some of this stuff up, or I'll graze on what's left until I won't be able to move."

Wordlessly, David helped pack up the leftovers and ferry them to the fridge. Cassie put their used dishes and cutlery in the sink and began to fill it with soapy water. David snagged the towel draped over the handle on the oven door and began drying.

"Well, aren't you the handy one?"

"Hey, Mrs. Michalek didn't raise her sons to be lazy bums."

"Her words?"

"The very same."

"I like your mother."

"She'd like you too."

As Cassie wiped down the counter with a damp cloth, he retrieved their wineglasses from the table. Handing hers over, he leaned his hips against the counter facing the sink. He casually crossed one ankle over the other and took a swig of his wine. Cassie propped herself against the opposite counter. She took a small sip of her wine, intent on savoring the last few mouthfuls.

Barely six inches of space separated their feet in the tiny galley kitchen, his in shiny, expensive black dress shoes; hers in the sexy, strappy heels. The contrast, masculine to feminine, held her attention.

She liked having David in her apartment, and not just because she'd imagined him here like this countless times. He'd been truly wonderful today. The way he'd swooped in to save her from herself during her tirade in HR had been, in hindsight, pretty spectacular. Then, as if that weren't enough, he'd spoiled her with takeout, made her feel a whole lot better about what had happened and, best of all, he'd listened.

She could hear Sarah McLachlan on the living room speakers, singing about sweet madness and the wreckage of a silent reverie.

"So," David said, setting his empty glass on the counter beside his hip. "What really sent Cassie Parker, Warrior Princess, into battle mode today?"

Cassie laughed ruefully at his phrasing. "It's kind of funny, actually."

"I'm all ears."

"Well, Amber..."

"Amber? You mean the soon-to-be-unemployed Amber?"

Even his joke didn't mitigate her embarrassment at what she had to tell him. "She, uh, she's been telling people that you and I are sleeping together. At work."

"I think I'd remember that."

"Yeah. No kidding. It's ridiculous, really."

"Why?"

"Pardon?"

The expression in his eyes was very direct, all hint of his earlier teasing banter gone. "Why's it ridiculous? Not the part about work, but the notion of us together as a couple?"

Cassie felt her breath leave her in a soft exhalation of surprise.

David pushed away from the counter and took the two steps that closed the gap between them. Gliding his fingers along her cheek, he bent close enough that she could feel the words on her lips as he spoke them. "Because I don't think it's ridiculous at all."

David's lips touched hers.

Chapter Seventeen

His kiss was soft, gentle. Other than his fingertips on her cheek and the inquiring glide of his mouth on hers, David did nothing to force her. She could have pulled away. Instead, all she could think was, *Finally.*

Thick, stubby lashes formed a sooty fan under his closed eyes. His skin looked warm. She put her palm on his cheek to see for herself that it was. The bristle of his afternoon beard felt pleasantly rough against her hand. David made a soft sound in his throat and canted his head to deepen the kiss. His fingers moved from her cheek to spear into her loose curls. His tongue flicked the line of her sealed mouth.

Cassie parted her lips and let him in. Their tongues met in a twining, mating of give-and-take that sent a pulse of sensation through her body.

He tasted of Asian spices and Chilean wine and a heady, masculine flavor that was all his own.

A broad palm slid from her hip to the small of her back. She swayed into him. His body, the lean muscles evident under the fine fabric of his clothing, quivered with restrained power. She felt his erection, harder still behind the zipper of his pants, press into her belly. Excitement blazed through her. She swiveled her hips in a subtle dance against him.

This time, David was the one who gasped. She caught the sound in her mouth, savoring it as his hand on her back pushed her more firmly against him.

Cassie lifted her other arm, intent on twining both around him. The weight of the wineglass in her hand stalled her. Blindly, she groped to set it on the counter. Then she allowed herself the indulgence of molding the strong column of his neck with her fingers, feeling the muscles and tendons move under her touch. The hair at his nape, so dark and smooth, felt as soft as she'd imagined.

David broke the kiss and she murmured a protest. He trailed his lips along the curve of her jaw, igniting sensations with teasing nibbles of his lips and teeth.

"Cassie." His breath blew warm and moist against her sensitive earlobe and she shivered. "Cassie, please say this is all right. If it's not, I'll back off. But please, just tell me what you want."

She leaned her shoulders away from him, far enough that she could look into his indigo eyes. His glasses sat slightly askew on his nose. She'd probably knocked them off-kilter when she'd run her fingers through his hair. Instead of silly, he looked like a tousled college kid, except for the hot gleam of his eyes behind the lenses. That gleam was all aroused, fully-grown male.

His hand roved up her spine, then down to the swell of her ass where her hips were supported by the edge of the counter. The fingers of his other hand flexed on her nape, as though resisting his intention to wait for her decision.

She smiled and plucked David's glasses off. Carefully, she set them on the counter with her wineglass. Then she draped her arms back around his neck.

"David. Can't you tell what I want?" She slowly undulated against him in blatant invitation. "I want *you*. Just you."

His answering smile was wicked and triumphant and full of erotic promise.

Oh boy.

If she'd been capable of thought, she would have considered his renewed assault on her mouth spectacular. She was too busy struggling with the buttons on his shirt. If she was going to do this—and hell yes, she was going to do this—she'd take what she wanted. David didn't protest. He cupped her jaw in both hands and ravished her mouth. She heard the distant *ping-ping-ping* as some of his buttons scattered to the floor. Yanking the sides of his shirt wide, she splayed her fingers on his bare chest. The slopes of his muscled pecs, sprinkled with hair, flexed under her hands. Quickly she found the hard points of his flat nipples and flicked them with her nails. He growled and pulled back to stare down at her.

His loosened tie dangled between the spread panels of his shirt, which she'd also managed to yank free of his waistband. Glasses off, dark hair tousled and the natural dusky color of his skin glistening in the single light by the sink—he looked like he'd stepped from the stage of a male dancer revue.

"Do that again," he rasped.

Panting, she said, "What? This?" She circled the pads of her thumbs over his nipples, then lightly scored them with her nails. He sucked in a breath. Bending her head, she lashed one with the tip of her tongue. His hands kneaded the back of her head as she switched her attention to his other nipple. She could feel his heart pounding in his chest. The thought that his nipples were as sensitive as her own made her breasts tingle in answering arousal. She trapped a masculine nipple with her teeth and tickled it with her tongue.

David groaned. "Two can play at that game," he said. Fisting his hand in her hair, he gave a firm but painless tug to move her away from his chest.

David's eyes roved down her body, taking in the formfitting black sweater and sleek charcoal skirt. The knit did nothing to hide her thrusting nipples. To avoid reaching for him, Cassie braced her hands on the counter on either side of her hips. David traced the sweetheart neckline with one blunt-nailed finger. He lingered in the hollow of her cleavage, which heaved as her breathing quickened.

He settled his hands on her hips.

"Take it off," he said. He didn't have to elaborate. She knew.

It was a bit of a struggle. He didn't move away or give her any more than the bare minimum of space she needed to cross her arms between them, grab the hem of her sweater, and slowly work it up her torso. As the fabric cleared her belly, he pressed his thumbs into her skin and began a slow, barely perceptible massage that sent the butterflies in her belly into some serious acrobatics.

Biting her lip, Cassie kept pulling until the sweater cleared her head. She dropped it to the floor.

David's attention moved to her bra, a delicate, highly impractical concoction of see-through black silk and lace that barely covered her nipples. His mouth hardened.

"Sexy as that is, take it off too."

A little amazed at her own daring, Cassie hooked her thumbs under the thin black straps. Ever so slowly, she ran her thumbs down. She skated her fingers over her breasts, then under. He watched with burning eyes as she lifted and squeezed, teasing him with her disobedience. Her thumbs rolled around her nipples. As she had with his, she scraped her nails over the sensitized nubs. Cassie bit her lip and moaned.

"God." David bent his head and enveloped one nipple and thumb in the hot cavern of his mouth. He sucked hard as he tongued her through the bra.

Cassie said his name in a weak, wispy voice. She pulled her hand out of the way. He nipped her through the silk and lace.

"Take it off," he growled. "I need to touch you."

Her resistance crumbled. "Yes. Okay."

Cassie's fingers trembled, but she still had enough dexterity to unfasten the clasp between her breasts. It gave way with a faint *click*. David nuzzled the cup out of the way, almost instantly sucking her bare nipple back into his mouth. Freed of any barrier, the pleasure intensified. Cassie ignored the bra straps caught on her upper arms and clutched at his head, urging him closer.

"Oh, God. Yes, David. Exactly like that."

He switched his attentions to her other breast and she cried out. He thrust his hips against her, and she cried out again, this time in frustration. Her skirt and his pants were in the way. She felt the iron length of his cock nudge the notch of her thighs, but it wasn't enough to ease the burning ache.

Her hands went to his belt. She fumbled with the buckle, somehow managed to work the simple clasp open. She undid the button on his pants and began to slide the zipper down. His hot mouth on her breasts made it hard to focus. The zipper stuck. Impatiently, she tugged at it. Stubbornly, it held. Without a qualm, she yanked the sides of the opening, as she had with his shirt. The zipper lost. Cassie didn't care. She thrust her hands into his pants, yanked the elastic of his boxers out of her way, and grasped his cock.

He jolted as though given an electric shock.

She glided her fist up in a slow, assessing pull. The skin of his penis felt warm and soft, silk over a steel rod of need. She reached the flange of the thick head and ringed it with her fingers.

David released her nipple and gasped, "Fuck, Cassie. That feels so good, sweetheart." He leaned his forehead between her breasts.

She rolled her palm over the head of his cock, feeling the wet precome on her skin. His breath huffed between her breasts as she began to work his cock. With her other hand, she reached farther to cradle his sac, gently rolling his balls in her fingers. He shuddered. She leaned over his bowed head and kissed his neck, loving the sweaty male scent of him.

Abruptly, David straightened and pulled her hands away from him. Without warning, he picked her up and set her on the countertop. Cassie let out a small yelp of surprise. He pressed a hard kiss to her lips. "Sorry, sweetheart. I can't wait anymore."

He put his hands on her knees and urged them apart. She tried to comply, but was stopped by the tight fit of her skirt. Undeterred, David worked the hem up until she could spread her thighs wide, exposing the lacy tops of her stockings. He settled between her legs with a satisfied groan.

He reached under her skirt and probed her with one finger. Cassie grabbed his shoulders as he stroked the sopping fabric of her panties where they stretched over her clit.

"These match the bra?" he asked, his voice sounding a bit strangled. He found one of the inner edges of the panties and pulled it aside.

She nodded. His fingertips grazed the throbbing kernel of her clit. Cassie's fingers clenched on his shoulders and she bit back a moan.

"You'll have to model them for me. Later." He said the last word as one finger pressed into her cunt.

Cassie squirmed in delight.

He pressed a second finger into her and fucked her with his hand.

"Yes!" Cassie tried to wriggle closer to him. She began to tremble uncontrollably. She felt the orgasm coming.

David took his hand away. She stared at him with dazed eyes. "Wait. What? What are you doing?"

David fumbled in his pocket. She couldn't quite see what he was doing. He bit off a harsh curse, then, "Thank you, God."

She saw he held his wallet. Flipping it open, he took a small foil packet from an inside pocket and tossed the wallet to the floor.

"Thank God is right," Cassie said.

He stared a question at her as he tore the packet open with his teeth.

"I'd hate to have to murder you for leaving me wanting," she said.

"Sweetheart, one thing I'll never do is leave you wanting." His eyes flashed over her, the heat in them as tangible as a touch. "Right now, though, I have to fuck you or stop breathing."

He unceremoniously shoved pants and boxers past his hips. Shirt flapping open, tie dangling, pants catching on muscled thighs—anyone else would have looked ludicrous. David looked delicious to Cassie.

She leaned back on the counter, gripping the edge with her fists, so she could survey him. His cock, long and thick, jutted from the dark curls of his pubic hair. She tilted her head and frowned as she examined the scar revealed on his right thigh. A strong feeling of déjà vu made her shiver. He had mentioned once in passing something about a car accident in college, but he'd never let on that it had been serious. That scar sure *looked* serious. Before she could ask about it, David gripped his cock. With quick movements, he rolled the condom on. She forgot all about the scar.

David reached for her. He drew her closer, ass sliding until she perched on the very edge of the counter. His hand went under her skirt. Deftly, he stripped the scrap of silky fabric down, moving just enough to free it from her legs and drop it to the floor. Then he was back between her thighs, spreading her wide as he used his hand to guide himself into position. The head of his cock touched her and they both moaned.

David stilled. "Cassie? Be sure. Be really sure this is—"

"David, stop talking and put that cock inside me!"

He bared his teeth in a fierce smile. "Yes, ma'am."

David shoved his hips forward, breaching her in one powerful lunge. Her drawn-out "oh" of pleasure earned her a hard kiss. He edged away, then plunged forward again. David hooked his arms under her knees, leaving her heel-clad feet dangling, and yanked her forward until she teetered on the edge of the counter. His hands cradled her ass. In this position, she had no leverage, could only accept his driving thrusts. She tried to brace herself against the counter with her hands, distantly heard the tinkling crash as she knocked her wineglass to the floor.

She was beyond caring, all her attention on David's pounding cock as he rocked into her, on the orgasm that was bearing down on her with all the subtlety of a freight train and on the cobalt-blue eyes blazing into hers.

Heat scorched Cassie's veins. Her belly tumbled like she was in a free fall. She tried to move her hips, but couldn't. It didn't matter. David seemed to know exactly what she wanted. He shifted his grip on her ass, tilting her lower body until every stroke of his cock rubbed across her clit. Cassie realized she was speaking, but didn't know what she was saying beyond a mindless chant of pleas and praise.

The single, clear word she spoke—shrieked—was his name as the orgasm stole her mind.

Her cunt clenched and clutched at his cock, milking the source of her pleasure with thorough force.

David shouted and shook. She felt his cock throb inside her as he surrendered to his own orgasm.

Clutching fistfuls of his short black hair, she covered his face with kisses. His hands kneaded her ass, and his hips continued to pulse against her as if he couldn't stop.

Finally, after what felt like hours, but was likely just seconds, David slumped against her. He buried his face in the curve of her shoulder, his gasping breaths stirring tendrils of loose hair that tickled her damp skin. She felt his lips move in a series of slow, gentle kisses.

He eased his arms from under her knees. Instead of pulling away, as she'd expected, he gathered her to him in a hug. Happy with his affection, she hugged him back, bracketing his hips with her knees and twining her calves around his thighs. She smoothed her fingers through the wet curls at his nape. His body put out heat like a furnace, making her want to purr like a contented cat. Well, for that, and for the best orgasm she'd ever experienced in her life.

"Why did you offer me the job?" The question was out before she realized it.

He stiffened like she'd struck him. Slowly, he straightened. His expression looked stricken before he smoothed it out. "What?"

She shouldn't have asked, but the question was out there, and she really wanted to know what his answer would be. "Why did you offer me a job with your company?"

He tried to back away from her. She tightened her thighs, holding him in place. He could have easily broken her hold, but accepted her unspoken demand that he stay.

"It wasn't so you'd fuck me, if that's what you're thinking," he said, his tone even.

"Good. I didn't think it was."

Some of the offended stiffness went out of him. "Then why'd you ask?"

"Because I want to know. And you still haven't answered my question."

"For all the reasons I gave you. You're intelligent, talented and ambitious. You have a lot to offer, and Stockton is wasting you on menial office work."

"Since I'm so intelligent, I should probably take the job then."

"Take the job. Don't take the job. It's your choice. I'll support whatever you want to do." His hand stroked over her tangled hair and he stared into her eyes. "The only thing you have to take, and keep, is me."

"Is that all?"

"Is that a problem?"

"Nope. Not from where I'm sitting."

She kissed him, gratified by how quickly his cock twitched to life inside her. He tilted his head and sank into her kiss. She tugged on his shirt sleeves. He obligingly shifted to help her pull his dress shirt off and add it to the growing pile of clothes on the floor. She left the tie. She liked the way it looked, a note of civility against the hedonistic beauty of his muscled body.

"Maybe," she said between lush kisses, "we should go," another kiss, "to my bedroom."

"Love to," he panted. "But we'll have to forgo doing certain things." He thrust his hips to illustrate his very hard point. "I just had the one emergency condom."

"Emergency condom?" She laughed. "Aren't you the good little Boy Scout?"

"Not exactly. If I was, I would have had a box of them. Sweetheart, believe me. I never expected tonight to go like this."

She gave him a wicked smile.

He chuckled and tweaked her nipple. "All right. Hoped, but not expected."

Glass crunched under his shoes. David frowned and looked down. "Let me carry you to your room and I'll take care of this glass. Your sexy shoes don't have enough to them to stop a stiff breeze."

She leaned close, nipped his earlobe and whispered. "I have a box of condoms in my night table. Boy Scouts aren't the only ones who can be prepared."

"Thank God."

Chapter Eighteen

David woke as Cassie snuggled closer, her slim but delightfully rounded thigh gliding between his legs. Just when things could have become more than a little awkward, she stopped moving and went lax in his arms with a contented sigh. Her head nestled comfortably on his shoulder as if made to rest there. He tipped his chin and stared into her upturned face. The bedroom was dark, but enough light made it through the half-closed shade that he could see she still slept.

The silvery glow traced the feathery crescents of her closed eyelids and brushed over her high cheekbones and lush lips. It flowed along the curves of her bare shoulder and tapered waist to the sheet draped loosely over her hip. Moonlight did wonderful things to a face that was lovely enough by daylight. Or candlelight. Or fluorescent office lights. Hell, as far as he was concerned, Cassandra Parker looked damn good anytime, anywhere. And she was clever, too, which really sealed the deal for him.

He cupped her shoulder and stroked his palm down her arm to cover her hand, the fingers of which were tangled lightly in the hair of his chest. In the moonlight, his skin contrasted darkly bronze against her pale milkiness. She murmured something indistinct and her lips tilted in a small smile, but she didn't wake.

He squinted in the direction of the clock. He could make out the blurry glare of the numbers, but without his glasses, he might as well have been trying to read a sundial in the dark. He thought it was probably late. The tiny apartment had the held-breath feel of the wee hours. Not so much as a creaking floorboard or groaning water pipe could be heard—which was rather a surprise, considering the age of the venerable old building.

The thought of drifting off again, wrapped around Cassie, her wrapped around him, was pretty satisfying. Almost as satisfying as sinking into Cassie's wet heat for the first time in the flesh in every sense of the word. He stifled a yawn, mildly amazed at his own stamina. He really should get some sleep, and let Cassie sleep too. She had to be exhausted.

In the morning, he'd take her to breakfast. Or make that lunch. Making love to Cassie in the morning light, arousing her to wakefulness with his hands and mouth, would be a great way to start the day. His mind supplied some pretty detailed images of that scenario. His cock began to harden, and he was faintly shocked. He'd been fairly confident the randy beast was done for the night. He wasn't exactly a teenager.

He forced the images from his mind and concentrated on the sleeping woman in his arms. Cassie was tired, damn it. Was it any surprise?

He wasn't an animal, and he didn't do his thinking with his dick. Now that he had her, he could afford to be patient again. He wasn't letting her go anywhere. She was his, and he was more than willing to be hers.

So let her sleep. When she woke, they'd have coffee, talk and decide where to go from here. Together.

He closed his eyes, determined to ignore his semihard cock and go to sleep.

Then he remembered the broken wineglass in the kitchen. It hadn't seemed like such a big deal when they'd knocked it to the floor the night before. There were so many more important things to think about. Like getting inside Cassie as soon as possible. Again, he forced the thoughts to the back of his mind so he wouldn't wake her up and take her, just because he could, and leave them both gasping and satisfied. Again.

But what if Cassie got up before he did? What if she walked into the kitchen barefoot, forgetting about the shards of glass on the floor, and hurt herself?

He'd better clean it up while he was thinking about it, just to be safe.

Carefully, he eased away from Cassie and out from under the sheet. She mumbled a protest.

"Shh. It's okay. Go back to sleep. I'll be right back."

He smiled at her moue, aware she wasn't awake enough to have made it consciously. Even in her sleep, she didn't want to let him go. Good.

He gathered the comforter they'd shoved to the floor during their last intense bout and gently spread it over her so she wouldn't get cold before he returned to bed. A fumbling search turned up his boxers, which he tugged over his hips. His glasses were in the kitchen. He should bring them back to the bedroom and leave them on the nightstand so he'd have them close at hand in the morning. As he left the room, he closed the door behind him as a final precaution against waking Cassie. Moving as quietly as he could, he paced down the short hallway to the living room.

And froze.

The glow that infused the room wasn't silvery moonlight. It was purple. And it seemed to be emanating like an angelic radiance from the exotic-looking woman curled up on Cassie's couch. He didn't need his glasses to recognize her.

"Jane!"

She waggled her fingers in a homecoming-queen wave. "Heya, David."

He shot a look at the bedroom door. Consciously, he lowered his voice to a rough whisper. "What are you doing here?"

"Oh, don't worry. I haven't been here all night, listening to you two lovebirds billing and cooing. Besides, our dear Cassie is out like the proverbial light. She wouldn't wake up if a marching band tramped through here. Although," she stared his body up and down appreciatively, "I'm sure she'd wake up for you if you put your mind to it."

He would have bet money on the fact he hadn't blushed in years. Still, he felt the tips of his ears heating up. "What. Are. You. Doing. Here?"

She pouted. "You don't have to be like that. I'm just checking up on things."

"Things?"

"Of course!" Her statuesque frame unfolded from the couch and she stood, clasping her hands under her chin like an eager schoolgirl. "So? Tell me. How'd you like your wishes?"

David thought of the past week, a sybarite's nocturnal nirvana, culminating in Cassie's final physical surrender to him tonight. His body responded as it had learned to do whenever he thought of her, but he couldn't muster a shadow of embarrassment that his reaction was evident to this strange, magical creature. He had, after all, gotten what he wanted: Cassandra Parker. "They were perfect."

"I knew it!" She wagged a finger at him. "Naughty boy. I knew you'd love them."

His smile faded. "There's just one thing."

"Hmmm?"

He sighed and ran a hand through his hair. "How do I know...how do I know it's real?"

"What's real?"

191

"How do I know what Cassie feels for me is real? That she cares for me, that it's not just sex to her. I'm not a knight, I'm not the ultrawealthy twin owners of a nightclub, and I'm sure as hell not a harem of triplet consorts from a set out of *Star Wars*."

She tapped her finger on her lips. "I don't really remember that scene from *Star Wars*."

When he just stared at her without speaking, she shook her head. "All right, simmer down. Yes, I know what you mean." She walked closer and put her hand on his shoulder. There was nothing remotely sexual about the gesture. If anything, it seemed almost maternal. She met his eyes. Her answer was so important to him that he barely noticed the silver and amethyst lights flickering in her irises.

"David, Cassie loves you. If she didn't, I wouldn't have been able to bring you two together. That's not the way this works. I can't make people feel things they don't. No one can. The wish to be together was yours, and the ideas for the fantasies came from Cassie, but there was one constant in all of them. You."

Relief washed through him. "So she won't expect us to have threesomes or foursomes or whatever? Because I can't share her. I'm not built that way."

She gave a little laugh. "For a smart guy, you still have some things to learn about women. But then, you are a man. David, what a woman fantasizes about and what a woman wants in the real world are usually completely different. Not always, but usually. Like I said, the one thing Cassie wants, no matter what, is *you*."

He thought about that for a moment. "Does she remember her dreams?"

"Bits and pieces. Certainly not from beginning to end. And she doesn't realize you shared them. Why should she? You won't have to worry about giving anything away by what you

192

say or do. The dreams are fading from her thoughts as dreams tend to do. Just like they'll fade from your thoughts. And your memories of me too, for that matter."

David frowned, uncertain if he was willing to lose what was, to him, something pretty important. The dreams were what had allowed Cassie to let go of her inhibitions and be open to a relationship with him.

Again, Jane seemed to read his mind. "Ultimately, it's not the dreams that are important. It's what the two of you do with reality from here on in." She cocked her head in a listening pose and gave him a feline smile. "Ah, well. So much for the marching-band crack. If I'm not mistaken, it's time for me to go. As the saying goes, my work here is done. Besides, I've got another project waiting for me." With her index finger, she made a come-here gesture. The perfume bottle appeared with a barely audible popping sound and hovered before her like an obedient hound.

It seemed a lifetime since David had spotted it in the window display of the strange little antique shop while on a business trip to Milwaukee. He still couldn't say what had made him go in and buy it, or why, when he'd touched a drop to his finger to see if it was something Cassie might like, he hadn't checked himself into the nearest psychiatric facility as soon as Jane appeared with all the subtlety of a thunderstorm and made her offer. Maybe it was because the contract with Stockton Enterprises was so near to completion, and Cassie seemed determined to keep a *No Trespassing* sign posted between them. Maybe it was because Cassie was so important to him that he was willing to try anything, no matter how crazy, to win her. Maybe it was fate.

"Oh, and one more thing."

Warily, he said, "Yeah?"

"Role-playing in the bedroom. I have a feeling Cassie will love it." Jane clasped the bottle and used it to flip him a jaunty salute. "I wish you and your sweet Cassie all the joy you can handle."

She snapped her fingers and was gone.

"David?"

He pivoted to see Cassie, a sheet wrapped loosely under her arms, standing in the bedroom doorway. She blinked sleepily and smothered a yawn with the back of her hand.

"What are you doing?"

"I was going to clean up the glass from the kitchen floor."

"How sweet." She craned her neck, trying to see around him. "Were you talking to someone on the phone? Or is the TV on? I thought I heard voices."

"You're hearing voices?"

"Ha-ha. Very funny. Call the men in the white coats."

He prowled toward her, glad she'd been so easily distracted. "What men? I could wear a white coat, if you like."

She went easily into his arms. She plucked meaningfully at the waistband of his boxers. "How about you wear nothing?"

"I can do that too."

She slid away from him and moved toward the bed, trailing the sheet like the train of a gown. The fabric dipped low, and he could see the line of her spine all the way to the upper swell of her buttocks. She dropped the sheet and crawled naked onto the bed.

That was enough for him. He stripped off the boxers. Cassie slanted him a heavy-lidded gaze over her shoulder and drank in the sight of him. Tilting her head, she said, "What made you decide to get a tattoo? I've always wanted to get one."

He smiled slowly. "Yeah? Can I make a suggestion as to location?"

She narrowed her eyes in mock anger and said primly, "Don't change the subject, David. Right now we're talking about *your* tattoo."

He glanced down at the quarter-sized black dragon beside his hip. "You really want to know about that now?"

She rocked a bit on her hands and knees. "Yes, actually. I think I do."

"Tease."

"Only if I don't follow through. The dragon?"

"It was a really stupid dare in college. Beer was involved. A lot of beer."

She stared at his middle and licked her lips. He didn't think she was looking at the dragon. "And?"

"We put on blindfolds and threw darts at a paper shooting target. Zak was on the marksmanship team and usually had a bunch around. Wherever the dart landed, that was where you had to get the tattoo." David put a knee on the bed. "Then we had to blindly choose a design from the tattoo artist's book. Turn the page and point."

He palmed her ass, enjoying the feel of her soft skin. Cassie's voice trembled as she said, "I thought it was against the rules or something. That you couldn't get a tattoo if you were drunk."

"Dunno. Steve knew a guy who knew a guy." He smirked. "You should see the tattoo he wound up with. On second thought, I'm never going to let you see his tattoo. You'll have to take my word for it."

He put his other knee on the bed and moved closer. Stretching, he was just able to reach over Cassie to the box of condoms in the drawer. The movement molded his front to her back. She purred and rubbed her ass against his cock. He thought of mounting Lady Cassandra on a fur rug in front of a roaring fire and wanted to growl in response.

He opened the packet and rolled the condom on with a trembling hand.

"Satisfied?"

"Almost," she said, and wriggled against him in carnal invitation. "Coming?"

The shattered glass, the genie in the living room, the responsibilities and challenges of a career he'd built from the ground up, what came next in this new, wonderful relationship—none of it mattered in this moment. Only she mattered. The woman of his dreams. His reality.

"Right behind you."

About the Author

Raina James has faced down deadlines and drama for twenty-plus years as an editor at a major Canadian newspaper. As an author of erotic romance, she gets to deal with...deadlines and drama, though in a much more fun way. On the home front, Raina is the mother of two boys and two girls, and overlord of a menagerie of pets that, if left unchecked, will rise up and rule the world. Or at least lay permanent claim to the couch. Raina loves to hear from readers. You can reach her through her website, www.RainaJames.com.

Her submission can heal him. His dominance can free her.

Impulse
© *2012 Moira Rogers*
Southern Arcana, Book 5

Sera Sinclaire is a New Orleans rarity: a submissive coyote trapped in a town overrun by dominant shapeshifters. Worse, she lacks the willpower to deny the alphas-in-shining-armor who need her soothing presence, even when their protectiveness threatens to crush her hard-won self-reliance.

The only shifter she doesn't want to push away is Julio Mendoza, a wolf so dominant he's earned a place on the Southeast council.

Julio doesn't have the luxury of indulging in the vacation his psychic shrink insists he needs. He can't turn his back on responsibilities he's beginning to wish he'd never shouldered. When an obsessive ex endangers Sera, though, instinct drives him to get her out of town. Watching her come to life outside the city makes him feel like he's finally done something right, and her touch ignites desire he doesn't want to ignore.

But soon, lighthearted flirting becomes a dangerous game of seduction, where every day spent falling into each other is another day avoiding the truth. Sera's ex isn't the only one who'd disapprove of their relationship. There are wolves who would kill to get Sera out of Julio's life—starting with his own blood kin.

Warning: Contains endless summer road trips, family drama, redneck werewolves, sexual power games and a taboo love affair between a submissive coyote who's among the last of her kind and a dominant wolf who loves his heroine's ass. Literally.

Available now in ebook and print from Samhain Publishing.

It's all about the story...

Romance

HORROR

www.samhainpublishing.com